SHADY LEWIS, born 1978, is an Egyptian novelist and journalist whose writing centres on cultural and political intersections within and beyond the Arab world. He lives in London, where he has spent many years employed by the National Health Service and local authority housing departments, working with homeless people and patients with complex needs. He has published three novels in Arabic to date – *The Lord's Ways* (2018), *On the Greenwich Line* (2019), and *A Brief History of Genesis and Eastern Cairo* (2021) – each of which engages with the social history of Coptic Christians and trajectories of migration from Egypt to the West, and a travel diary, *Death Tourism, or a Comedy of Foreigners* (2024). *On the Greenwich Line* has also been translated into German, French and Italian; the French translation was shortlisted for the 2023 Prix de la littérature arabe.

KATHARINE HALLS is an Arabic-to-English translator from Cardiff, Wales. Her critically acclaimed translation of Ahmed Naji's prison memoir *Rotten Evidence* was a finalist for the National Book Critics Circle Award for autobiography, she was awarded a 2021 PEN/Heim grant for her translation of Haytham El-Wardany's *Things That Can't Be Fixed* and her translation, with Adam Talib, of Raja Alem's *The Dove's Necklace* received the 2017 Sheikh Hamad Award. Her work has appeared in *Frieze*, *The Kenyon Review*, *The Believer*, *McSweeney's*, *The Common*, *Asymptote*, and others. She is one third of teneleven, an agency for contemporary Arabic literature.

ON THE GREENWICH LINE

Shady Lewis

Translated by
Katharine Halls

PEIRENE

First published in 2024 by
Peirene Press Ltd
The Studio
10 Palace Yard Mews
Bath BA1 2NH

ISBN 978-1-908670-95-3

This book is a work of fiction. Names, characters, businesses,
organizations, places and events are either the product of the
author's imagination or used fictitiously. Any resemblance to actual
persons, living or dead, events or locales is entirely coincidental.

Designed by Orlando Lloyd
Cover illustration by Nick Dahlen

Typeset by Tetragon, London
Printed and bound by TJ Books, Padstow, Cornwall

This book has been selected to receive financial assistance from
English PEN's PEN Translates programme, supported by Arts
Council England. English PEN exists to promote literature and our
understanding of it, to uphold writers' freedoms around the world,
to campaign against the persecution and imprisonment of writers
for stating their views, and to promote the friendly co-operation
of writers and the free exchange of ideas. www.englishpen.org

Supported using public funding by
**ARTS COUNCIL
ENGLAND**

ON THE GREENWICH LINE

For Ulrike and Maria Wadia

Let the dead bury their dead

(LUKE 9:60)

1

He was a full twenty years younger than me. Other than that, I still didn't know much about him. Indeed, a few days earlier I hadn't even known he existed. It's not unusual to be unaware of certain other people's existence in the world; of most people's, even. But the fact that I was now responsible for his body, so suddenly and out of the blue, was bound to cause me some anxiety. Death was going after people half my age, and without any preliminaries at all! Still, that in itself didn't bother me more than listening uneasily to death counts on the morning news. I think what horrified me beyond all else was the way he'd died. How dismal to die like that, and at that age: in one's room, quietly, lying on the bed, without even one person to witness what had happened. It wasn't a death that seemed well suited to our times. For better or worse, we seem obliged to take death seriously these days, to consider it an unmitigated evil that can't be justified or understood.

The poor guy might have died in slightly grander fashion. In a way that wouldn't have been so hard on his loved ones. He could have met his end alongside a few other people; even if nothing had tied them together but their shared death, at least he would have had some company, which is not nothing. In fact it's been very popular lately. Or he could have died in front of a few witnesses, so the details of his final moments, recounted again and again, could have brought some comfort to his family, or added just that bittersweetness necessary to keep his memory fresh and vivid for as long as possible. His death could have been preceded by some sort of suffering. Then it would have been seen as deliverance, bringing relief to those around him. At worst he could've been killed in a car accident or something like that. Even that sort of senseless cruelty is a thing of some consequence, and provokes a gasp and a hand clapped to the heart in those who hear about it, followed by a shake of the head at the absurdity of fate...

None of this would have made much difference to the deceased, it's true. As far as we know, the dead don't suffer from the cruelty of death anywhere near as much as the living. Those sorry souls are expected to gather up the severed parts of whatever's been destroyed by the dead person's departure and carry on living as if nothing at all has happened. It's a miracle more impressive than birth and no less tragic than death itself.

I was an especially unlucky living person, who, by some twist of fate, had been given the arduous task of experiencing up close the death of a person entirely unknown to me. I couldn't blame anyone but myself. One night, around midnight, I'd got a call from Ayman in Cairo; that was the start of everything. I could have refused outright to get involved. I could simply have said no, or wriggled out of it with one of the little lies I'd got into the habit of using since

I'd come to live in London, but you can't underestimate embarrassment and the things it'll make you do.

It was the first and only time Ayman had come to me needing something; in fact, nobody from Cairo had asked me for a favour of any kind since I'd left. This was my first chance in ten years to prove that my being in London had some purpose or was of any use to anyone. It was a combination of hubris and shame, and it was bound to lead to disaster.

After a short opening gambit in which he assured me that I wasn't obliged to help him, and that he'd understand completely if I said no, Ayman asked me to go the following morning to a hospital in East London, collect the dead body of a twenty-year-old man, and make arrangements for his burial. That was it. He didn't give any further details.

'It's a direct request, and I need a one-word answer – yes or no.'

Ayman's voice was firm, and I could see there was no point trying to sway him, but I did my best anyway.

'That's not fair,' I said. 'Can't you tell me who it is first, what the situation is?'

As expected, all this achieved was an even firmer response. 'If you can do us this favour, I'll tell you what I know,' he replied, 'but if not, then there's no point chewing your ear off. So? Yes or no?'

Ayman got the answer he wanted with no trouble at all; within thirty seconds of picking up the phone I'd agreed to do it. His winning card wasn't the frosty note I could clearly hear in his voice. It wasn't the closed question, either, with the minimal, condensed answer it required – a tyrannical simplicity no question had ever held before – that wrested my assent out of me.

It was my curiosity that did it. Ayman wouldn't have told me the story of the deceased if I'd said no; I'm sure he'd have punished me rigorously and never mentioned the dead young man again. He knew curiosity was my weak point, and he exploited it ruthlessly.

Despite the intrigue of the request, the excitement fizzled out completely as soon as Ayman started to explain. Any thrill of enlightenment that went through me didn't last more than a second or two. As usual, once the secret was spoken, all cause for curiosity evaporated. It didn't surprise me: in general, I find that knowing things, for all that people get excited about it, is overrated and boring.

To tell you the truth, the story of the young man, Ghiyath, would have been more exciting if it had happened, say, ten years ago. Or if it hadn't been so intensely repetitive. If it had ended with some unforeseen outcome or been crowned by a more heroic death. In fact the story was quite dull, and quite disappointing, to the point I can scarcely now remember more than its broad outlines. Ayman was acquainted with a Syrian family who'd moved into a small house next door to his mother's home in their village. This might have been the most interesting detail in the whole story, because I couldn't imagine how any Syrian had ended up in the village of al-Tayyibin in Upper Egypt, a place you'd struggle to find on a map to begin with.

Anyway. The family had fled Syria when the war there got worse. The fact they'd ended up in Egypt was proof they were either exceptionally unlucky or desperate. Meanwhile, their only adult son – Ghiyath – had stayed in Syria for the sole reason that he was locked up in one of the security regime's prisons; which one, I can't remember, not that it would add anything to the story. According to Ayman, Ghiyath and two cellmates had dug a tunnel a hundred miles long using plastic spoons, a tunnel that traversed the line dividing regime and opposition territory. Yet no sooner had he climbed out of the tunnel than one of the opposition factions arrested him for some reason or other (no surprises so far). For the three weeks he was detained in opposition territory, control shifted back and forth between twenty-two different factions (or twenty-three? I'm not sure). A sharia judge allied to one of the factions condemned him to death for reasons uncertain, but the judge himself was executed half an hour later. And so the late Ghiyath escaped certain death.

The story then gets tediously bogged down in labyrinthine details: how he survived forty-one air raids carried out by aeroplanes from twenty-one different countries; the regime's barrel bomb assaults; gas attacks, both the coloured and colourless kinds, the kinds that have a powerful stench and the kinds that are odourless; and that's without even mentioning the Katyusha rockets. By pure chance Ghiyath experienced this whole assortment of horrors while barely more than a child.

That he ended up in yet another security facility only adds a further layer of repetition to the narrative. Certainly the methods of torture used at the prison oblige us to recognize the singular talent and imagination that must have gone into inventing them, and to appreciate the zeal and commitment shown in their application. But in the end these things all achieve very similar results. Ghiyath dug himself another tunnel, longer than the first, to get him out of the country altogether; he dug alone, and without the help of any cutlery this time. But I think Ayman was probably exaggerating when he claimed Ghiyath had done all this with hands tied behind his back.

On his nineteenth birthday Ghiyath finally emerged out of the tunnel at the seashore, and swam from Beirut to Alexandria in a mere three days; apparently a friendly dolphin accompanied him on the journey and kept a vigilant watch the whole time. But unluckily for Ghiyath, that summer day wasn't the most propitious time to arrive in Egypt, because for various convoluted and trivial reasons, Syrians had suddenly become unwelcome. But here he finally had a stroke of good luck in that the Egyptians put him on the first flight out of the country. The plane flew round in circles for a few days, looking for somewhere to drop him off – somewhere that would agree to take him – before finally landing in Ecuador. Why not?

Ten months went by. He travelled through four continents and fifty-seven countries on foot, sometimes alone and sometimes in company; stayed in forty-three camps; crossed two oceans, four seas and thirteen rivers; and escaped certain death multiple times. An earthquake struck in Guatemala, an alligator tried to eat him in Bolivia. He'd have drowned off the shore of a Greek island had he not held on tight to the dead body of a child which was floating beside him. After that he was chased by a police dog in Bulgaria, which came within an inch of tearing his heart out and chewing it to pieces. A fellow Syrian set him on fire in Berlin. The most dangerous near miss of all was in a public park in Hungary: he was running away from the police when a female journalist tripped him up, sending him headlong into a sharp rock that almost sliced him in two. But a rascal lives long, as they say.

I'm not saying there aren't interesting parts here and there in what Ghiyath went through; the problem's just that these days it's all very familiar. There are a million similar if not identical tales, and ultimately these things get boring. Not to mention that some aspects of the story – which I won't reveal out of respect for his memory – are fairly reprehensible. Ghiyath committed a number of unlawful and dishonourable acts in the course of his long journey. Granted in most cases he was forced to, but the ends don't always justify the means, particularly when it comes to lying. For example, when Ghiyath finally made it to this little island of ours, he claimed – to avoid being sent back to France, where he'd come from – that he was a minor, aged fifteen. Amazingly, he was such a good liar that the authorities were prepared to believe he was a full five years younger than he actually was.

It might sound like I'm being a bit hard on him. I wouldn't be surprised if people put my attitude down to some kind of hostility towards refugees, and I understand; there are many immigrants in a similar position to myself who've arrived in this country, or wherever else, and immediately wished they could close the door behind them and throw away the key. But that's absolutely not the case here. I have an unimpeachable position on refugees, which I arrived at by a rough and thorny path, and at a remarkably young age. Perhaps I ought to tell the story and justify myself.

At the dead end of the side street in eastern Cairo where I grew up lived twin boys, who were one year older than me and much taller. They were an unusual-looking pair: aside from their bright red hair, they had pale faces so covered with freckles you could barely make out their features. And they acted as strange as they looked, always seeming to have some mysterious excuse to avoid playing or talking with the other kids in the street.

That mystery was reason enough for us to feel a combination of fear and disgust towards them, the way a person feels towards strangers. But the gulf that lay between the twins and us was destined to be broken, by a method of their choosing, and, unfortunately, at my expense.

One summer's evening, I was sitting on our front doorstep. The street was totally empty, as it usually was around that time. In the distance I glimpsed Ashraf and Sharif, the twins, walking confidently towards me with a look of malicious intent. I didn't imagine they'd try anything right in front of our house – it would be unprovoked, and far too audacious – so I guessed they just wanted to get a rise out of me.

I was wrong. One of them came up so close behind me that his knees nearly touched my back, and stood towering directly above my head. When I looked up, he spat a huge ball of phlegm straight into my eye. The other followed it with a kick in my side, and I let out a scream of pain and humiliation. The pair sauntered away in the direction they'd come from, satisfied with their achievement, until one of them turned back and shouted with an anger I couldn't comprehend: 'Blue-bone scum!'

The insult put an abrupt stop to my wailing: the 'unprovoked' attack now made sense. Only because I was a 'blue bone' – an easy target, let's say – could they pick on me without fearing the consequences. Knowing that calmed me down. The strange lesson I learned at that young age was that many injustices feel more bearable if you can only understand their logic; the worst are those that defy explanation. I don't know why injustice should be less painful when it comes with a few clear general rules. Maybe because you know what to expect, or because it loses its individual valence and you don't feel like it's aimed at you personally. That ball of spit was aimed at all Christians, not necessarily at *my* eye, that's what I told myself. The thought was satisfactory, and relieved me of any thoughts of revenge.

My mum didn't share this view. I hadn't been expecting much from her; usually, when it came to blue bones – or black bones, my own invented retort – I knew she preferred quietism. 'Haven't I told you not to play with those bloody Muslims?' she would always say. 'Well there you go, now they've given you a thrashing. Serves you right!'

I always knew to expect a slap around the face when I stubbornly replied, 'Like there's anyone else!'

This time, though, some kind of miracle intervened. The normally meek and downtrodden woman, taken over by a supernatural outburst of fury, grabbed me forcefully by the arm and dragged me the length of the street to the twins' house. She screamed hysterically and thumped at the door. When the twins' mother answered, she pushed her roughly aside and the woman tumbled to the ground. My mum stormed through the house, me following in her wake, until she found the two boys in the living room, where she set about slapping and kicking them so indiscriminately I worried she might accidentally kill one of them. That might have been what their mother was thinking too, because she was out in the street, shrieking to the neighbours to help her. My mum's deranged fit only lasted a minute or two, then she left the house, her body heaving with rage, yelling at the top of her voice for all the street to hear: 'So now we've got refugees coming over here and beating our children? We're in our own country and the beggars we let in are spitting in our faces!'

Refugees. It was the first time I'd heard the word, and to make matters more confusing, my mother kept alternating it with 'Palestinians' in her furious ranting; it seemed to me they must be the same thing. But whatever that word meant, whoever they were, the most important thing – and this thought filled me with pride – was that they came below me on the ladder of getting thrashed. In fact, they came below everybody, because I myself was on the last step but one.

'Mum, what does "refugees" mean?'

'It means people with no country.'

If I'm honest, it was the first time I'd experienced a childish sense of belonging to my country. And I began to feel a sort of affection towards refugees, because thanks to them I no longer had to be everyone's punchbag.

Things didn't end there; the next developments were dramatic, and mortifying. After two hours of calm, which my mother spent in a state of high alert, the twins' father came home from work and found out what had happened. The fearful silence in our house was broken by the man's angry banging on our front door. 'Now Christians are beating our children, are they?' he thundered.

My mum was shaking with fear as she opened the door. The man did exactly what she had done in his house: pushed her aside, knocking her to the ground, and strode through to the living room. He wasn't looking for me, as I'd thought, but for the man of the house. 'Don't you have a man to keep you under control?' he roared.

Luckily my dad wasn't back from work yet, so there wasn't much the man could do; he could hardly lay a hand on a woman. After trying to smash some of the furniture but only hurting his own hand, he stalked back outside to interrupt my mother's yelling, which was directed at the men of the street: 'The Palestinians are coming after us in our own homes and you're watching from your balconies like a bunch of women!'

The man's reaction took me by total surprise: he burst out laughing, shaking his head from side to side like he couldn't believe what he'd heard. His anger seemed to have faded completely. 'Who's Palestinian, you crazy bitch?' he said as he walked back towards his house, slapping his palms together in incredulity.

There were no further scuffles between the twins and me, and no confrontation ever took place between their father and mine, who made sure to leave and enter the house as inconspicuously as possible for the next few days. But my mum's misunderstanding only took a few minutes to clear up. Once the fracas was over, the assembled neighbours told her that Ashraf and Sharif's family were neither Palestinian nor refugees; they were Upper Egyptians who had once lived in Suez, then fled during the Six-Day War and been resettled in Cairo. Maybe that was why she'd got mixed up.

As I grew older and came to grasp the full dimensions of the story, I adopted a clear position towards refugees, and in this regard I won't have anything said against me: refugees must be treated with equality and respect. You might think someone's a refugee and later find out they're not, which can lead to embarrassment; or worse, they might turn out to have a father who's prepared to thrash your father, and that is downright dangerous.

Back to Ghiyath, before we forget his story. The things that happened from the time he arrived in the UK up to the day his housemate noticed a terrible smell coming from his bedroom aren't worth going into. The Polish man hadn't remarked on Ghiyath's three-day absence; in the time they'd shared the flat, they'd hardly spoken more than two words to each other, just yes and no and some improvised sign language as required by the daily upkeep of their affairs. The body was bloated and lying on its back, looking peaceable and uninterested. The housemate called the police, who took the body to hospital for a post-mortem, and there they determined that the cause of death was either disappointment, or exhaustion from working more than twelve hours per day, or perhaps just the sudden anticlimax of there being no immediate danger of death.

'God rest his soul, Ayman,' I said. 'What's it all got to do with me, though?'

The story had left me struggling to maintain the enthusiasm I'd been feigning so far, but Ayman wasn't going to let me get out of it. 'Are you trying to go back on your word?' he asked accusingly. 'We've already agreed you're going to pick up the body and sort out the funeral.'

That wasn't exactly what we'd agreed. All we'd said was that I'd help.

'Is it that simple?' I asked, trying to find a way out. 'Aren't there procedures? Doesn't it have to be a next of kin or something?'

Here Ayman struck the fatal blow. 'Don't worry about that,' he said. 'Everything will be ready for you by tomorrow evening.'

My attempts at backtracking had failed; Ayman had all the answers, as usual. A British consular official in Cairo had called the family of the deceased to inform them of his death and offer her heartfelt condolences for their tragic bereavement. She suggested they apply for an emergency visa so they could come to London and bury the boy. She was kind and solicitous and even hinted that they might not be obliged to return to Cairo afterwards; it was an opportunity they shouldn't pass up. But she immediately apologized for the suggestion: how could she be so indelicate as to raise the issue of seeking asylum in the UK immediately after informing the family of the dreadful news? She reiterated several times how sorry she was to have characterized the boy's funeral as an opportunity. The family accepted her apology straight away, and by the end of the call, Ghiyath's father had found himself, almost without realizing, making an appointment to come to the embassy the next day with his entire family to fill out the visa application forms and begin whatever procedures were required for them to travel to the UK.

There must have been a slight misunderstanding, though, because the family showed up at the embassy in a pickup truck carrying their suitcases and other belongings; everything they owned, in fact, which in any case wasn't much. On their way there the driver expressed surprise they were taking so much luggage with them to their first visa appointment, mocking their naivety in not so many words. But they had a convincing answer: it was the first time they'd lost a child, and they didn't know what you were supposed to do. And it turned out they weren't so mistaken. The blonde employee who received them was even more sympathetic than the one they'd talked to on the phone, and informed them that the consul himself had taken an interest in the matter, and had he not been on the phone to London following up on the case right then, he would have come to give them his condolences. The family filled in some forms and handed in their passports, and within an hour of arriving the employee asked them to leave, with a promise that they'd get a call at the end of the day or the next morning to tell them they could pick up their passports.

The thing was that until the point the family left the embassy, they hadn't had the chance to take in the news they'd received or make sense of what they were doing. The previous day, after the consular employee had called them, the mother had spent the whole day packing their bags and cleaning the house, because it wouldn't do to leave it dirty when they left. The father was busy too; he barely put the phone down all day, calling acquaintances from here and there and trying to scrape together the money for plane tickets and other costs.

As for the death itself, they'd both managed to pretend it hadn't happened. In fact, the mother, who hadn't shed a single tear since they'd got the news, had been possessed by a very strange conviction. She held fast to it although she knew full well it was absolute insanity. She'd left behind a seventeen-year-old boy who couldn't even boil an egg, and yet he had survived all those horrors and somehow managed to get himself halfway across the world. He couldn't possibly have died such a pointless death after all that. It had to be some trick he'd dreamed up: feign death and bring them to Europe. On a Skype call he'd told her he was starting an application for a family reunion visa, and that they'd soon be able to join him. Also, it wasn't the first time he'd faked his own death – he'd done that twice so far, at least. The ease with which matters proceeded at the embassy only confirmed her theory.

For a few moments, the father was blindsided by the truck driver's insistent questions. The guy had been waiting over an hour and wanted to know whether he was meant to take them to the airport or back to al-Tayyibin. The first option was sarcastic, obviously. His tactless joke didn't help Abu Ghiyath, who stood, mutely staring back at him.

After a long silence, the mother intervened and asked the driver to drop them off with their luggage in Tahrir Square, because the embassy might call back and it would be best if they weren't too far away when they did.

Ayman happened to be exiting Sadat Metro station just as the driver was unloading the family's luggage from the truck. He was on his way to work, and for some reason he stopped and glanced back towards the Mugamma' building instead of heading straight down Tal'at Harb Street as he usually did. That was when he spotted the man and woman standing, surrounded by suitcases and children. It was one of those little coincidences that set in motion a chain of unforeseen, logic-defying events, like so many other things about this story. If there's anything that can be concluded from that brief turn of the head at that precise moment in time, it's that chance goes about its business with painstaking rigour and precision.

He went a little closer to be sure it was them, and saw instantly from the way they stood that something bad had happened. The first thing that came into his mind was that they'd been kicked out of their house, or had to leave for some other reason. At that time, the security services were systematically visiting properties and ordering landlords to evict Syrian tenants, or else doing the job themselves.

'Abu Ghiyath, what are you doing here?' said Ayman.

The man stood rooted to the spot and his eyes widened when he saw Ayman, though his grave expression didn't change. It looked like he was trying to say something but couldn't: his mouth was open, but all that came out was a hiss that ended in a faint hoarse rattle. Ayman tried to help by repeating the question, but it didn't do much, probably because Abu Ghiyath hadn't had a chance to think about what he was doing there. After a couple of moments more, the younger children started to cry quietly and tug at their father's arms, terrified to see him in this state. Ayman looked at the woman in the hope she might provide an answer to his question, which he repeated a third time. That was when Umm Ghiyath burst into a long howl of grief and started slapping her face with all her might. Then she rounded on her husband, grabbed him around the neck and screamed something in his face that Ayman couldn't make out. That was finally enough to rouse the man, who quickly shook off her grip and clapped a hand over her mouth. Passers-by were already turning to see what was happening, though luckily none had stopped.

Ayman was very distressed at this scene and took a few steps back to give the man and his wife some space. He was tempted to quietly slip away; his presence obviously wasn't helping at all, in fact his question seemed to have set them off. But then Abu Ghiyath, who still had a hand over his wife's mouth, turned to Ayman and told him with an unexpected and unnerving composure that by God's will Ghiyath had died, and that they were on their way to London to bury him.

He had to head off quickly to be in time for a meeting at work, but Ayman felt awful for making his excuses. Once he'd heard why they were waiting in the square, he advised them not to draw attention to themselves, because it was dangerous being Syrian in Egypt in those days, and even to be noticed at all. By that he meant that the woman should stop crying, which is what she finally did after her husband told her several times to get a grip.

Around five, Ayman heard that after he'd seen the family, the embassy had indeed called them back and asked them to return to pick up their passports – without a visa. The consul himself was waiting to meet them this time. He looked exceedingly embarrassed and apologized repeatedly: the decision wasn't his to make, unfortunately. He intimated that he would like to assist them in repatriating the body so the burial could take place in Cairo, but that it would cost a considerable sum. The other option was for them to designate a representative in London to arrange for a burial there. In that case, all they would need to do was provide the embassy with the details of the designated individual and sign two forms. The man was terribly kind, and implied that he favoured the second option, which would cost the family nothing, and undertook to have the paperwork done that same day. The consul was so tactful he even apologized for raising bureaucratic and financial matters in such circumstances. Abu Ghiyath was unable to respond. All his wife could do to help was to ask the consul to give them until the next morning to think about it.

The family spent the night at Ayman's flat in Sayyida Zaynab, and that was when Ayman called me. The boy's father couldn't sleep; he was still trying to take in everything that had happened. A few hours earlier he'd been making preparations to fly his family to London, never to return, and now he was trying to understand what sense there was in a death such as this. He was accustomed, or inured, to news of death; he had no choice. Even head-on, it had become a straightforward matter for him and many others: his mother and two brothers had died in two separate air raids and he had personally gathered up what remained of their bodies, piece by piece. His wife's sister had gone missing and her body was found torn up by the roadside. His cousin and his small family had all drowned; his childhood best friend had died under torture and he was afraid to be seen at his funeral. Uncles, acquaintances, cousins, childhood playmates, in-laws, colleagues, former neighbours, school friends: they'd all died monstrous deaths, one after the other, sometimes several on the same day. They were all on the list of the dead, in any case. But what was the sense in a person going through the trauma of survival so many times, only to die a death like that, at twenty and without a scratch on them, lying on their back, alone and an outsider, with no killer who could be the object of revenge or even, at the very least, hatred?

The father couldn't think any further than that. The burden of deciding what came next then fell to the mother; it was her who'd asked for the extra time, anyway. She tried to chase from her mind the thought that she would never see Ghiyath again, even dead. She tried to forget that there was a bureaucrat in some government office somewhere in London who had never met her and who knew nothing whatsoever about her son, not the painful caesarean section by which she'd given birth to him nor the tears she'd cried when she looked into his tiny face for the first time, and that this person had decreed she would not attend Ghiyath's funeral. With one signature they had simply and effortlessly deprived her of the chance to kiss her son's face for the last time, and to reassure herself of the cold presence of death in his body. How terrible, the simplicity with which these things were decided! And what death could be worse than this? For death to become, for those in their situation, simply a lifeless body: a body to be disposed of, appropriately where possible but dictated by a limited range of choices governed by cost and feasibility and well-intentioned promises of assistance from strangers – sincere promises that most likely couldn't be kept.

'The living will be here longer than the dead, Umm Ghiyath,' said Ayman, a note of severity in his voice. 'You should save your money for the children.'

That settled it. She said nothing but nodded in defeat, which Ayman took as her assent to the second option. The boy would be buried in London. He would have two funerals, one there and one in Cairo, which Ayman would take care of himself.

'I've got to organize a funeral for him?' I exclaimed. 'I can sort the burial, fine, but a funeral...'

It looked to me like I was being asked to pay the price of Ayman's chivalrous promises to the boy's family. He didn't pay me any attention. 'Figure it out,' he said, brushing aside my objections. 'It can't be that complicated.'

'Yeah, right, I'm sure it'll be no hassle at all,' I replied, feeling like sarcasm was the only path left.

Ayman brought the call to an end sounding more decisive than he had done at the beginning. 'Don't be funny,' he said. 'This isn't the time. It won't be that hard, and I'll have the power of attorney with you by tomorrow afternoon.'

I was completely and utterly ensnared.

2

He was twenty years older than me. He'd left for Italy, on one of those boats that dump their human cargo several kilometres from shore, and I hadn't seen him since. Once he got his papers and found a legal job cleaning toilets, he visited Egypt twice, but for some reason I didn't see him on either visit. I hardly remembered what he looked like, just that he was skinny; his voice I couldn't remember at all. But six months after arriving in London I heard it once again.

The uncle who never kept in touch had rung my mother for a catch-up two days earlier, and she'd told him the good news that I'd just got my first job after months of searching. Feeling obliged to congratulate me personally, he asked my mother for my number. It was a long call. I was a boy of ten when he'd last seen me, and he wanted to know everything that had happened in the intervening period. I wasn't up for that, so I gave him a dry synopsis of my studies and work, which seemed to satisfy him. What really took a long time was his astonishment at the nature of the job I'd managed to obtain.

My uncle – actually a first cousin once removed – could barely believe his ears. He repeated each of his questions several times. Every time I answered, I could hear a faint gasp of amazement on the other end, and I couldn't help laughing, though I tried hard not to. Although struggling to believe me, he was overjoyed, and yet somewhere in this mixture of delight and incredulity there was also a note of embarrassment, perhaps because his questions began to sound increasingly envious as the conversation progressed.

'Let me get this straight,' he said, enunciating the question clearly just to be sure. 'You work for the government?'

'Not exactly, Uncle. I work for the local council.' I tried to downplay it, but it didn't work.

'So you work for the government. I mean, what else is a local council? It's part of the government! And you really work in an office?' His voice was twitching with awe. All I could do was go along with him.

'That's right, Uncle.'

Silence.

'And do you have your own desk and chair and so forth?' he asked, more seriously now.

I tried not to let my annoyance at his insistent questioning show in my voice, but I couldn't find it in me to feign enthusiasm when I replied that yes, I did. 'I have a computer as well,' I added.

Uncle was positively jubilant at this achievement by a member of his family in the diaspora. 'Mashallah! And you've only just arrived there! Tremendous! Mashallah!'

'It's only a junior position,' I said, making another attempt to keep things in perspective, though I knew it was futile. 'Still, thanks be to God.'

He wasn't having any of it. 'Junior my hat!' he exclaimed reproachfully. 'You have your own chair. A chair for you to sit on!'

Over the next nine years, the memory of that phone call, and Uncle Tanios's eager questioning about my chair and the fact of my sitting on it, kept me from losing my patience with my job time and time again. It really wasn't a bad job. True, I'd thought of it as a stepping stone to begin with, but even so, I was luckier than many. Living in London, working for a local authority, working full stop – that was a lot of luck. And to be fair, the thing I disliked about it was the same thing I'd disliked about other jobs in the past: there was nothing to do, or very little. Back in Egypt, I'd always had to pretend to be working; here, that wasn't necessary, because everyone around me was always so engrossed in their work they barely noticed my presence. I couldn't work it out: how were they constantly occupied when I couldn't find anything to do? My previous bosses had often called me lazy. The issue now, though, wasn't filling the time but looking for things to do that I could convince myself had some meaning. And so I had to keep reminding myself of that phone call with my first cousin once removed, every day and on difficult days more than ever: I have a chair, and I sit on it.

Things had improved since the Tories had come to power and social housing funding was slashed in half. The service managers at the various local authorities had got together and come up with a brilliant idea for dealing with austerity: as budgets decreased, so paperwork would increase. We would fill in more timetables, write more reports, attend more meetings. We couldn't provide any services, since there was hardly any social housing left and a million people were on the waiting list, but we could increase the paper trail and lengthen processing times to a few years. As time ticked by, and application processes inched their way to completion, council staff would be occupied and *necessary*. Data would have to be collected and entered into the system, then checked and reviewed every so often, then rechecked and inputted into tables and charts; then updated data had to be collected and compared with the previous data, and so on. Likewise, this long-winded administrative process sustained applicants through years of living in temporary accommodation and permanent poverty. Nourished by a combination of faith in the welfare state and wishful thinking that the process would produce the desired outcome, they remained hopeful throughout; the emblem of their hope was the yellow application form. This wasn't a new idea. It had been the logic of bureaucracy since time immemorial: I once read an interesting book about Ancient Egypt – its name escapes me now – which confirmed my theory. The Pharaohs, it explained, only undertook vast, pointless construction projects like the Pyramids of Giza in order to keep the populace busy during flood season, when there was no agricultural work to be done, and to make sure they didn't start asking existential questions, or having midlife crises, or thinking thoughts, or generally get up to any of the mischief a person with too much time on their hands is likely to get up to.

*

The day after the phone call from Ayman, I was finding it more difficult than ever to draw reassurance from the conversation with my uncle. All I could think about was the body and the funeral; I'd only got two hours' sleep and I wasn't in the best of moods. So when I saw the email in my inbox, it was the last thing I needed: *Home visit with mental health team 11 a.m.*

On an ordinary day, this wouldn't have been an onerous task; I was always glad to get out of the office and stretch my legs, and there was a certain drama to seeing a mentally ill person who'd just been discharged from hospital and listening to their ramblings, which always involved some tall tales. On the odd occasion we got a difficult one, I didn't have to do much; my presence was a formality more than anything else. It was the practitioner from the mental health team that had to do everything, assessing whether the patient was capable of living independently and if they had any additional needs which would qualify them for priority access to social housing. I must say they were very good at all this, even if they probably shared my view that their role in the whole thing was merely a formality, since there was barely any social housing to be had and the results of the assessments thus meant very little. In most cases the service user would have a nervous breakdown and get sectioned again, or attempt suicide to escape the interminable waiting and the misery of temporary accommodation. When they were successful, there would be a huge row between us and Mental Health over who was responsible. They'd blame us, saying that the 'tenant' should have been placed in permanent accommodation; our managers would counter that the 'patient' was not being adequately cared for in the community and should have been admitted to hospital. Despite the superficial differences of opinion and the game-playing with terminology, it was noticeable that both sides had a deep faith in buildings. And rightly so: every social ill can be remedied by the right building. Crime can be eradicated by prisons, illness by hospitals, the ravages of old age by nursing homes, youthful rebellion by school, poverty by social housing, and so on. Unfortunate issues really only arise when a person is placed in the wrong building, or when there isn't enough space for them in the right building.

Thankfully, I didn't need to trouble myself with any of this. It was only the most senior staff who were responsible for the complicated business of shuffling people around and matching them with buildings. It was their job to arrange transfers from hospital to prison, or school to office, or factory to old people's home, or prison to social housing, until the person in question killed themselves or died of natural causes, thereby freeing up space for the next person who was to be saved.

In short, there was no reason to worry about the visit scheduled for that morning, other than that I don't like surprises. I prefer the general outline of the future to be laid out in advance, at least at work. The email had come from the generic Mental Health address, rather than a specific staff member. From long experience, I had good reason to mistrust messages that came from impersonal sources. Usually their aim was to sidestep some problem or other or evade responsibility, shifting it to the nominal but shadowy entity that was the 'service'. Sometimes they were a show of force, designed to intimidate the recipient for some purpose: correspondence that came from the 'service' seemed unassailable and invited no reply. On a couple of occasions, I'd tried calling the phone number in the email signature and asking to speak to whoever wrote the email, or to the 'service', but I'd never got anywhere. Nonetheless, I took a deep breath and called the number to find out who would be conducting the visit with me.

A secretary picked up. 'What difference does it make?' she asked, in a hostile tone which seemed unwarranted by the situation. 'Any of the mental health team could do it. That's how it works across all the services, isn't it?'

She sounded like she was about to lose her temper. I'd clearly called at a bad time.

'I'm a bit OCD, you know what I'm like!' I joked. 'Will you have a look at the timetable? Just for my peace of mind.'

She exhaled slowly, like I'd made a very unreasonable demand. 'Fine. Let me see... For some reason there's no name here. It'll probably be Pepsi or Ludmila. That help your OCD?'

I let out a long, huffy sigh of my own, in revenge. 'Not really, but thanks anyway.'

She put the phone down before I'd finished the sentence, but that was OK; she'd told me what I needed to know, and hearing the names Pepsi and Ludmila had cheered me up.

Pepsi was the weirdest person on the mental health team, and my favourite. Pepsi was her real name, and her surname was even stranger. Not that McMillan was a strange name per se; it was just that, to me, it didn't seem to go with her Caribbean accent and black skin.

The first time we'd met, she told me apropos of nothing that her great-grandfather had indeed been Scottish, and her great-grandmother one of many enslaved people on the plantation he owned in Jamaica. With the same nonchalance with which she'd told me this, Pepsi then asked me what my race was. I was thrown, partly because the question was rude, but also because I had no ready answer.

'North African,' I blurted. It was the first thing that came into my head.

Pepsi stared back at me, visibly insulted. 'You're not African,' she said aggressively.

She had a cheek, I thought, but I made light of it. 'You seem to know more about me than I do,' I said jovially. 'I'm from Egypt. Which is in Africa.'

Rolling her eyes, she smiled mockingly. 'You're not African. I am, but you're not.'

'Have you ever been to Africa?' I asked, raising my voice despite myself.

'No, never,' she said breezily, ignoring my derisive tone. 'But I'm still African. You wouldn't be even if you spent your whole life in Africa.'

There was no point trying to talk to her, but I couldn't resist the childish invitation to argue.

'Says who?'

'Me.'

There was a silence. I tried a different tack.

'Well, if you know everything, then you tell me what race I am.'

'I've no idea,' she said, 'but you're definitely not African. If you're not black then you can't be African.'

Our conversations always ended at a similar point. It was nigh on impossible to get the better of Pepsi in an argument; she simply imposed what she thought on everyone around her. It was her who convinced me to dye my hair after it started going grey when I was thirty. She made fun of me relentlessly, telling me I looked older than her. She was right: Pepsi was sixty, but she could have been in her thirties. She was slightly taller than me, with a strong, athletic figure. She wore bright colours and drove a sports car, and her voice was loud and vivacious. The day she brought in a tube of hair dye and forced me to put it in my pocket, I realized I'd entered her world. Pepsi was obsessed with dyeing things, especially human things. What one immediately noticed about her was the thick layer of white powder that covered the skin of her face, arms, legs – indeed every visible part of her body. At first I was hesitant to ask about it, thinking it might have been a treatment for some sort of skin condition, but then one day I spotted her standing at a bus shelter, casually crushing a piece of chalk – regular blackboard chalk – between her fingers and spreading it on her face. So I plucked up the courage to ask, and although the answer she gave was complete nonsense, I found a certain madman's wisdom in it.

'You must think I'm nuts. But you don't know what it's like being black in this world. You have two choices: either you adapt and make your skin white, or you laugh at them. Two solutions, one more extreme than the other. If you try the first one, everyone will laugh at *you*, but you have to keep going, a new layer every day until it looks like the real thing. I've gone for both solutions: I'll assimilate, but I'll make a mockery of them while I do it.'

After that, our relationship became much deeper; in many ways, she reminded me of my mother. But I did begin to wonder about the bottle of hair dye she presented me with every month. Did she really want me to try to look younger? Or was it meant for my skin, to give me a taste of what it was like to be a real African in this world? I didn't dare ask.

Ludmila was Pepsi's negative. She was in her late twenties and looked it, but she talked like a woman of retirement age and was as indifferent as it was possible to be about everything, up to and including life itself. She also had her own race complex, but inverted. Ludmila, you see, was the only white employee on the mental health team; the rest were all people of colour to some degree. And she knew as well as we all did that our job – clearing the rubble of society, sometimes looking for survivors underneath it and other times colluding to keep them buried – was not something any white person would be caught dead doing, much less down here on the lowest pay grade. The only exception were people from Eastern Europe, like her, who were as desperate as the rest of us. And so she laboured to remind herself that she was white, and blonde no less, by addressing everyone she worked with, service users and colleagues alike, with a distinctly superior air.

This was good reason to dislike her, and I did, until the day she decided to dispense with the formalities. After finding out on one of our joint home visits that we were both reading the same novel by the same Czech author, her cold manner evaporated and she asked me to join her for lunch at her favourite cafe. So I did, and instead of the allotted one hour, we stayed for two, most of which she spent complaining. About everything: the country she came from, London, her poky flat, literally everything. I nodded along, bored but feigning sympathy, until she really opened her heart and began to complain about the job we did. Only then did I detect a flare of anger in her blue eyes, which were otherwise as cold and still as a lake.

'It's a waste of resources,' Ludmila said, sounding as poetic as she did heartfelt. 'We're torturing those poor souls when they'd be better off dying in peace.'

I thought I must have misheard. 'Sorry, what was that?' I asked hopefully.

Her eyes flashed again. 'You know what I mean,' she said. 'It's not society's job to carry that burden.' She sounded more enthusiastic than I'd thought her capable of. 'We should let nature do its job. Tidy things up. The people who deserve to live are the ones who can stand on their own two feet and don't need benefits or council houses.'

'Why are you doing this job then?' I asked. I was trying very hard to give her, and myself, a way out, but she firmly turned down the offer of a face-saving retreat.

'Bad luck,' Ludmila said. 'I couldn't find anything better. I have to pay the bills, just like you.'

My first reaction was a faint shudder and a desire to throw up. I was having lunch with a woman who worked with defenceless, mentally ill patients, whose very job was to safeguard their welfare, and she thought they should be left to die.

But then something unexpected happened. I was gawping at her, trying to take in what I was hearing, when she leaned forward and brought her mouth to my ear. 'I've scared you, haven't I?', she purred, seductive yet steely.

I nodded as a shiver of arousal ran up my back. My heart was pounding so loudly I was sure she must be able to hear it, and I had to pull my rucksack onto my lap to hide a sudden, painful erection. She noticed, and leaned back in her chair, looking smug.

'Good.'

It was our little secret. We never talked about it again; we simply pretended it hadn't happened. More than once, I thought about reporting her for what she'd said, but there was no point. She would have denied it, and it would have been my word against hers. And she was actually a very conscientious worker. She'd probably just needed to let off steam that day; she'd surely never do anything to hurt any of her service users. Even if she wanted to, she wouldn't be able to. Perhaps the only virtue of the many rules and regulations of bureaucracy is that it restrains individual inclinations of this kind and stamps out any personal opinions which do not accord with the governing approach, just as it restrains inclinations of other kinds, even the most honourable. But what discouraged me above all from reporting her was my fear of dousing the blaze of pleasure I felt whenever I saw her, or even thought about her. Of course I felt simultaneously guilty. I didn't know if the guilt was a result of the pleasure, or the pleasure a result of the guilt.

I have no explanation for any of it, other than that there is something exciting and sexy about evil. I think I was so exhausted from doing battle with the world that I simply fell supine before the forces of ill. Or maybe it was submission itself that was sexy. There was no hope of the relationship ever leaving the realm of fantasy, because Ludmila had returned to her former reserved manner, and if anything was even more supercilious with me than previously. We both knew that would turn me on more, but an implicit agreement between us placed limits on where things could go, and so my desire remained unquenched and undimmed.

The chance I might see Ludmila on the visit began to excite me. I was on the verge of drifting off into one of the daydreams that regularly ate up my working day when I realized I only had fifteen minutes to prepare for the visit and leave the office. I might not have an important role in the visit itself, but I had to be acquainted with the case (and when we said 'case', what we meant was the service user; sometimes we referred to them by their health condition, but I found 'case' more neutral, on balance). The email had copious attachments, which we called 'case literature'. And literature it was:

> *'Derin attended today wearing bright clothes and in high spirits. Explained it is Newroz. Smiled throughout the appointment, including when I asked re: side effects of antidepressants and when I gave prescription. Informed*

43

me she would not need to continue medication for very long. I advised her not to discontinue medication without prior consultation with me.'

'First visit. Tenant A was in a state of extreme agitation. It took half an hour of shouting and crying before she could tell me what the problem was. She stated that she could not wait any longer, that her life is "temporary" and "one long wait" and that every wait leads to more waiting. When she arrived in London, she waited years to obtain refugee status. Her first application was refused and the court was slow in responding to her appeal. She then had to wait again before she could apply for settled status. She had to wait before she could move into temporary accommodation and was then notified she would have to wait to be entered on the system in order to wait for permanent accommodation. She also stated that she had to wait for either her husband or herself to die so that he would stop beating her. After forty years, he died, but it didn't stop, because her son and his wife then started beating her. She counted the days in prison, and then had to wait again to be released from hospital. Again and again, someone would inform her she had to wait. Tenant stated that everyone filled in yellow forms and asked her to wait.'

'Ms A. 65 years. Nationality Turkish. Speaks Kurdish and very basic English. In UK for ten years. Granted refugee status three years ago. Negative experiences in her home country. Referred to social services by GP in December 2015 due to social isolation and domestic abuse by son.

Ms A did not engage with the care plan offered to her and communication was extremely difficult even with the help of an interpreter. Ms A was arrested in March 2016 on suspicion of deliberately setting fire to her son's house and received a 9-month custodial sentence for arson later that year. Prison requested an urgent medical assessment and asked for her to be transferred to a secure hospital as her mental health deteriorated rapidly over the first two weeks in custody. Ms A suffers from auditory and visual hallucinations which tell her to harm herself and others but is able to manage symptoms with medication. Ms A was discharged when her mental health improved and is currently in temporary accommodation pending move to permanent accommodation. She is unable to live with her son and cannot afford the private rented sector. Ms A is physically capable of taking care of herself. She is a heavy smoker, which presents an increased fire hazard. She does not have friends or relatives in London. Current living situation is having a detrimental effect on her mental health and it is essential that she be moved to permanent accommodation as soon as possible.'

'Patient has a personality disorder. Her mental health has recently deteriorated. She claims her son and daughter-in-law are abusing her physically, although there is no evidence of this. Her son informed us that she has threatened to set fire to his flat. Patient presents a moderate risk to herself, others and the public, but has no history of carrying out threats. Currently no further measures necessary. Family should continue to observe her.'

'Derin presented complaining of recurring nightmares. She sees huge birds hovering in the air which drop balls of flame on her. She escapes by jumping from mountain to mountain, and when she thinks the birds have lost sight of her, she is attacked by birds coming from the other direction. Nightmare appears to be related to traumatic events she experienced in Turkey and then Iraq after her marriage.'

'Current temporary accommodation is not suitable for this tenant. It is a basement room, poorly ventilated, with mould. Does not meet health and safety requirements. Tenant should be rehoused as soon as possible. Please note the above comments were also made in our last report three months ago. We have so far received no response from your service.'

I didn't have time to read everything; the woman's file contained a vast number of notes, reports, prescriptions, court orders, Section 2s and 3s, solicitors' letters and police reports. It was enough material to write a trilogy of average-length novels. But over the years I'd spent at the council, I'd acquired various skills for dealing with case literature and could now intuit which reports were important merely by glancing at their first and last lines. I could hone in on relevant paragraphs without needing to read the full document; the number and distribution of these paragraphs depended on the type of document and who had written it.

In most cases I could make a good guess at the author's identity without looking at the details on the file, just as avid readers can detect the style of their favourite writer from the first paragraph of a novel. Each service had a house style, and conventions which were unconsciously passed from one generation of employees to the next. The different professions, too, had their own narrative techniques, and each brought a different set of emotions and concerns into their writing. Most importantly, each had a jargon which was impenetrable to outsiders. For example, I could tell a psychologist from a psychotherapist within two lines: the first was more formal, and interested in diagnosis and testing, while the second referred to the patient by their first name, took an interest in their past, and foregrounded tragedy. I could likewise tell a social worker from a housing officer in the space of three sentences; both were concerned with rehabilitation, but the former paid more attention to the law, while the latter thought anybody could be reformed by a well-ventilated east-facing property. At first glance, a psychiatrist's report often appeared identical to a police report, and it would take me a careful reading of at least two paragraphs to distinguish them. Generally speaking, both were hostile to the person in question, but the former was sufficient to detain a mentally ill patient against their consent, while the police usually could not do so without a court order. There were also personal eccentricities that had nothing to do with the author's profession. The report that mentioned Derin's 'bright clothes' could only have been written by Dr Kumar, the GP; nobody else had his classical style or his sense of the poetic.

Nothing about the case caught my eye. It contained the usual mix of trauma, language barriers and communication issues, domestic violence, bureaucratic delays, poor inter-agency coordination and the inevitable culmination in psychiatric hospital or prison – in this case both. The case file also didn't tell me much about the service user, because it was as inconsistent as you'd expect of something written by ten different people from ten different standpoints. There was no way of telling, for example, whether the service user was indeed a victim of domestic abuse, or whether her accusations against her son were a result of her hallucina-tions; no one could even say for certain what language they had been made in. This was why the council's databases would have made such an excellent historical source: they were utterly contradictory, like everything in history. But what was interesting was the funny sense I got as I was scrolling through that the service user was somehow delib-erately exploiting the chaos around her to force all these support workers and specialists and doctors and council bureaucrats to write about her, albeit in a language she barely understood. It was as if she knew a life so shattered could not be put back together, and all she could do was give some meaning to her misery by dragging other people into it, or at least forcing them to record it. When Service User A's life ended, a litany of her sorrows, hardships and nightmares would remain saved on the system, along with the colour of the clothes she had worn on Newroz and the birds that appeared in her dreams. And maybe one day someone would read through it all, and remember her, and feel a little of what she had felt.

These thoughts were swirling in my head as I picked up my bag to leave the office. A gust of warm air hit me

as I stepped out onto the street, and I felt pride, even ela-
tion, at the task I was about to perform; I was the means
by which this poor woman would be granted a certain
immortality, or what in the office we wittily referred to as
'administrative posterity'.

3

I had to put the address into Google Maps. Service User A lived in one of the hostels that fell under my remit. I visited two or three times a week, and I knew it took around ten minutes to walk there; but there was no point trying to get there by memory alone. Although I'd lived and worked in the borough for a decade, I still struggled to find my way around; even making my way to places I frequented on a regular basis felt like navigating a hall of mirrors. Far from improving, the problem seemed to get worse as the years went by. I was forever mixing up street names and places, and I couldn't put a name to my feelings or even tell them apart. And there were so many houses. Long lines of them with their tiled peaked roofs, in identical colours and proportions. There was no escaping their insistent, repetitive presence. You could turn right, turn left, cross the road, get on a double-decker bus and stare out of the upper deck windows, wander through a park half-daydreaming, and still all you'd see would be the same design. The same overbearingly precise template repeated again and again, in street after street, neighbourhood after neighbourhood. London, like so many cities, seemed built for workers. The factories were gone, but the place still had the soul of a factory, and its ghosts roamed the city.

The wisdom behind the Victorian terraced house was that orderly, symmetrical city streets would inspire a humble and compliant temperament in their residents. The price, whether by design or as an unintended side effect, was tedium. The Victorian house was the magic cure-all of its time: bureaucratizing the visual landscape, it functioned to accustom both eye and spirit to routine and make monotony the natural order of all things – time, space, the visual environment, the working day. And endless repetition is indeed restful, since it harbours no surprises, gives no pause for thought and excites no anticipation. It does not arouse troublesome ambitions or thoughts of escape. And for all that monotony has a bad reputation, it is equitable if nothing else. Each house is the same as its neighbour; each street looks like the next. Any individual can be replaced with another, or with a machine if need be. Any corner of the city can be turned into a house or a place of work, and conversely any building can be knocked down or replaced without anyone feeling a thing. Childhood memories, say, can be substituted or forgotten or slotted into some other time or place with the same ease with which people move house or emigrate, without the least regret and without anybody around them registering their departure.

So that day, as soon as I got out of the office I was instantly confused as to whether I should go left or right. The internet was being slow, and my maps refused to cooperate for at least a minute; only when my phone rang was I finally extricated from this small-scale humiliation.

'Stay where you are! I'm on my way! I'll be at your office in five minutes and we can walk to the hostel together.'

It wasn't Pepsi or Ludmila. The voice on the other end of the phone, which bubbled with vitality, punctuating its words with unwarranted but perfectly natural peals of laughter, was Kayode's. I was surprised; Kayode had been appointed lead psychiatric nurse on the mental health team four years ago, and he'd never accompanied me on a home visit before. As far as I was aware, he didn't even do public-facing work, other than in emergencies or exceptional cases. Service User A's file didn't suggest she required any special treatment.

In any case, Kayode's announcement he'd be accompanying me certainly aroused my curiosity. I saw him regularly at the quarterly reviews which brought together representatives of the various health and social care divisions. We usually sat next to each other, quietly keeping a safe distance from our more enthusiastic colleagues, who took themselves too seriously and inevitably drew attention to the lack of enthusiasm of those nearby. Kayode's approach at these meetings was to smile broadly, revealing his gleaming white teeth; this filled me with an irresistible feeling of affection and familiarity towards him. When he found himself obliged to say something, typically because someone had criticized him or accused his department of incompetence, his response was unique. He never attempted to defend himself; instead, he would launch into a comprehensive theory of society inspired by some tiny detail he'd picked out of the conversation, and finally, with a sermonizing flourish, his Nigerian accent tempered by long years spent in London, he'd finish up with a set of general pronouncements about life which in sum didn't necessarily hang together but were each reasonably wise in their own way. Apart from that, Kayode spent most of those meetings playing with his mobile under the table, swiping his finger across photo after photo of grand houses with swimming pools. I never knew what the story with the houses was; was he planning to buy one, or was the point just to stare at them wistfully? Perhaps today I could ask him.

Kayode appeared in front of me suddenly, with a sprightly skip that seemed out of keeping with his towering frame and pot belly. He threw one arm around me, rubbing my shoulder heartily with his other hand like we'd just returned from battle.

'Hello there, my favourite man!'

This didn't mean anything; it was how Kayode greeted everyone he knew.

'What happened?' I asked. 'Where are Pepsi and Ludmila?'

He took hold of my forearm and set off. 'Come with me and I'll tell you everything on the way.'

As he walked, he began to explain what had happened, without looking me in the face.

'They had an argument this morning and wouldn't get on with their work. I tried to intervene, and they both got angry at me instead. Pepsi shouted at me! It was the strangest thing I've heard since my school days. She said I always took Ludmila's side against her, just like my ancestors sold her grandmother to the whites. She said we Africans are unscrupulous and always willing to sell out our own race. I had to laugh. There was nothing I could say to that. Then Ludmila accused me of the same thing. She said "You lot always stick together." I asked her what she meant by "you lot", and she said I should stop acting innocent when I knew exactly what she meant. So I gave her a piece of my mind. I said, "You're not white, sweetie, you're black too. Everyone who does this job is black, so you'd better stop kidding yourself."'

'You told her she was black?' I started to laugh, picturing the look on Ludmila's pallid face as Kayode's words sunk in. 'I bet that didn't go down well.'

Kayode shook his head; it wasn't that. 'She was more annoyed I called her sweetie. She said she'd make a sexual harassment complaint against me for using demeaning sexist language. But she couldn't argue with the fact she's black!'

I could see he was on the verge of coming out with one of his entertaining social theories, so I followed the unusual direction of our conversation.

'But Kayode, she's not black. She's actually very blonde. You know that.'

'No, she's black,' he answered. 'We're all black here.'

'Not all of us. What about Liam? He's white and he's got ginger hair.'

'He's Irish, therefore he's black.'

'What about Alan? He's English.'

'Communist. That makes him black.'

'OK, what about Dee? She's not Irish or a communist.'

'She's a lesbian and she grew up in care. Double black.'

'What about me then?'

'You're Muslim, and Muslim is black.'

'I'm not a Muslim, you know that. My family are Christian.'

'Makes no difference. You look Muslim, and Muslims are black.'

'What, a person can "look Muslim"?'

'Of course! At least, they can here. Everyone who's not white is a Muslim.'

'OK, so Chinese people are Muslims?'

'No, Chinese people are black.'

'So you can be black without being Muslim.'

'Sure. If you're Chinese.'

'But basically what you're saying is that there's nobody at all who's white.'

'Exactly,' said Kayode. 'Real whites are very rare. You might live your whole life in this city and only glimpse one or two of them. You might not even notice them, unless you're very observant. But don't forget, black people aren't all the same. There are black Blacks, Eastern European Blacks, Chinese Blacks, very black Blacks, half-and-half Blacks, Muslim Blacks and black Muslims, Blacks by choice, and Blacks by coincidence or bad luck, Blacks in disguise, crypto-Blacks who are something else in public, part-time Blacks, full-time Blacks, Blacks who are white on the inside, like coconuts, and Blacks who are white on the outside, like... I don't know. All to say, it's very complicated.'

Kayode wasn't joking, and he wasn't even using the terms 'white' and 'black' as social signifiers; as far as I could tell, he held what he was saying to be true in the most literal sense. He actually told me Ludmila's skin was getting darker. He was of the opinion that a white person could gradually become black, it was even fairly easy – though a black person could never become white. Only in cases like ours, he said, could Blacks become white, and that was by returning to the countries they came from. Kayode exclaimed that anyone with a swimming pool in their house was *categorically* white, and sooner or later, he too would become white when he bought the villa in Nigeria, replete with pool, that he planned to retire in, thereby joining the ranks of another category on his list: the white retiree Blacks.

He was so deeply engrossed in explaining his racial theories that we reached the hostel before he'd had time to tell me who was going to interpret for us. When the mental health team had phoned Service User A to arrange the visit, using a Turkish interpreter, she'd apparently insisted she didn't speak Turkish. When they called back with a Kurdish interpreter, she told them the only language she spoke was Arabic. They didn't believe her, and I didn't know whether or not they'd booked an interpreter in the end. Maybe they just expected me to interpret.

We arrived at the hostel five minutes early for our appointment. This ought to have given us enough time to sign in at reception, but the glass cubbyhole at the main entrance was empty and the door propped open. After a few moments of confusion we heard the porter calling to us to come straight into the building, and a buzz as the front door opened. We couldn't see where his voice was coming from, but he told us he was in the boiler room because there was an issue with the thermostat and the building was too hot. It was summer; the central heating shouldn't have been on at all, so he was trying to fix it.

As we stepped through the doorway we slammed into a wave of heat. In a long corridor, lined on both sides with rooms, residents loitered in their underwear. A gaggle of half-naked boys lay on the tiled floor, and two infants were crying while their mother yelled at them to shut up. I glanced through one of the open doorways and saw a pregnant woman standing on a chair, trying to get her head through the bedroom's tiny window for a breath of air. Kayode caught the expression on my face. 'Poor thing,' he said, shaking his head sadly. 'She won't manage it. These windows all have bars on the outside to stop them killing themselves.'

Then we heard a woman's voice shouting something in an incomprehensible language, followed by a long wail.

There was a small staircase at the end of the corridor that led to the basement, which housed several further bedrooms including Service User A's. A pair of teenagers sat on the bottom step, whispering, and gave us a faintly hostile look as we made our way past them. They followed us with their eyes until we stopped at the door of the room. 'That woman's mental!' shouted one of the teenagers. 'Sort her out! She cries all night, we can't sleep.'

Kayode knocked at the door, ignoring them, then took two steps backwards so I was standing in front when the woman opened the door. The room was tidy enough, but it smelled mouldy and the one window was closed. The woman was wearing several layers of winter clothes and a scarf. Droplets of sweat ran down her face and made a distinctly audible sound as they hit the floor.

I briefly hoped that the woman didn't in fact understand Arabic, and that we could turn on our heels and go. The heat was stifling, and from one corner of the room came the loud mechanical hum of a motor somewhere behind the wall. I thought I might faint. But then the woman's face, which had been glowering when we entered, lit up as I greeted her in Arabic. She invited us to come in, using a mix of broken Arabic – an Iraqi dialect, I thought – and English.

There was only one chair, so I asked her to sit on the bed and offered the chair to Kayode, who had paperwork to fill in. I told her I was happy to stand. I was about to explain the purpose of our visit when the woman, who was looking Kayode up and down in distaste, turned to me and said angrily, 'What's the slave doing here?'

My heart leaped; if she was going to use racial slurs, then we'd be out of this blazing hellhole in no time! I told her firmly that we did not tolerate that kind of language and that she would have to apologize or the visit would be cancelled. At that she started shouting and waving her arms in Kayode's face. He asked me to translate what was happening. I didn't want to tell him she'd called him a slave, so I gave a watered-down version: she wanted a white employee to look at her case, because they were the only ones who could help her and put an end to her long wait. I concluded my translation by saying it looked like the visit was over, because she was refusing to take the assessment he was meant to conduct, and turned towards the door.

'Patience,' said Kayode, gripping my arm. 'Tell her I'm head of the team and there's no one more senior than me. I'm here to help her.'

I refused at first, but he insisted, and spent ten minutes cajoling the woman, the broad smile on his face irritating me more than anything else. It looked like the visit would last longer than I'd thought.

Kayode took out his laptop and began explaining the aim of the questions he was about to ask. The assessment, comprising a number of simple puzzles to test her memory, focus, ability to synthesize information and various other mental capacities, would take twenty minutes. The results would determine whether or not she could live independently. If she could, she would qualify to be moved to permanent accommodation in the near future. There was no need to worry, said Kayode; she looked fine to him, and the test was standard procedure. All she had to do was answer the questions to the best of her ability.

But the assessment wasn't as straightforward as Kayode thought. The elderly woman struggled to understand my Arabic, and her thick accent was difficult for me to follow too. The mother tongue she refused to speak kept seeping out, imposing itself on her pronunciation of both Arabic and English as if she had the soul of some other language entirely. Thanks to my many years of dealing with accents and their owners, I had methods for reaching through the layers of languages imprinted on each one and locating the fossils buried within. I usually managed to strip away the distortions caused by the memory of a native language the speaker had failed to erase, which burdened their tongue and caused them nothing but pain. The accents I'd encountered all seemed to me to be a present trapped inside the accretions of the past; the more one could harden one's heart and shed those memories, the purer one's accent and the more confident one's articulation. Learning a new language, contrary to what people may think, depends not on memorizing new things but on forgetting the old. Clearly Service User A's past weighed heavier on her than her present; there was no clearer proof of this than how she spoke.

Every time Kayode put a question to her, she would burst out laughing. The answers were hilariously self-evident and yet also confusing, like anything very simple. Several times she covered her face with her hands in embarrassment, to hide the childlike mirth in her eyes, while Kayode looked on with a reassuring smile and noted down her scattershot answers, which I attempted to translate. The first question was about the time; her answer to this was that she came from the mountains and mountain people didn't wear watches, but she could confidently say the time now was slightly before noon. When Kayode pressed her for an exact time, she replied nonchalantly that it was either three or five. As for the date, she'd stopped keeping track of the days since she got out of prison, she said, because all days seemed the same to her and she'd rather it stayed that way. She knew it was a Friday, because her neighbour always knocked on her door to ask her to go to mosque (she always refused). But Kayode wasn't having this, because although it was correct, it was the answer to the wrong question. He'd asked for today's date, not the day of the week.

For my part I tried not to be too faithful when translating. When he asked, for example, 'Who is the prime minister?' I rephrased to give her a clue: 'Which female politician leads the government?'

She stared at us for a few moments. 'The Queen,' she announced triumphantly. The disappointment in our eyes was visible. 'I don't understand politics,' she muttered defensively. 'I just want a flat.'

Kayode pressed earnestly on, despite the rivulets of sweat making their way down his forehead – the woman had refused my request to open the window several times – the beatific smile never leaving his face. He didn't seem troubled at all.

Next, he produced a set of cards from his briefcase with a flourish. They had pictures of an animal on them, each of which he asked Service User A to identify. They both seemed to be enjoying the game.

The woman became more and more incredulous as she examined the pictures first of a unicorn, then of a kangaroo. Shrugging in resignation, she told me she'd seen these animals on TV but didn't know what they were called in Arabic or English, or any other language. Faced with Kayode's determination to get an answer out of her, any answer, she laughed, pointed to the unicorn, and said, 'Lion.'

She flicked through the cards in her hand, picked out the kangaroo and glanced at it, then turned to my colleague and for the first time answered confidently in English: 'Donkey.'

The kangaroo had brought us to the end of the assessment, and Kayode asked for a few minutes to enter the answers on his laptop. But it took longer, because the internet wasn't working, so I had no choice but to listen to the woman telling me about her past. She was born in the south of Turkey, and at the age of sixteen had moved to Iraq with her husband, who was half-Arab. She'd witnessed two massacres, one on each side of the border, and told me a couple of details about one of them which I can't recall, because it was so hot I was feeling faint and could barely concentrate. I was keen, though, to ask what her first language was. At first she wouldn't say, but when pressed she told me her mother had nursed her from birth on Kurmanji. When she moved across the border, she had to learn the language of the land. It was hard on her soul to be parted from the language whose milk she had suckled, and made to speak another. She told me that souls only speak one tongue, the one learned in childhood; the mind may grasp others, but they never reach the heart.

'Why won't you speak Kurdish then?' I asked.

'That's different,' she said. 'Don't think I'm denying my roots. There's nothing happy about our past, but at the end of the day it's *our* past. We possess it like it possesses us. You can't be truthful here and survive. You have to lie to avoid death, or at least not open your heart to strangers. You understand. When someone opens their mouth and speaks to you, here in exile, in the language you miss and long to hear, your heart drops its defences and your soul pours out before them. But if you want to lie, then it's easiest to do it in a foreign language. So I speak Arabic with you in order to lie. In any case, speaking a strange tongue is the soul telling lies.'

I was about to ask more about this philosophy of hers when Kayode stood up abruptly. Frustrated with the internet connection, he announced that the visit was over. The woman leaped up from her perch on the bed, rushed to the door, and caught hold of his arm. 'Tell me what will happen to me!' she beseeched him. 'Please. I can't wait any longer.'

Kayode tried to extricate his arm, but her grip was much stronger than her thin frame and gaunt face suggested.

'I won't let you go until you tell me if I'm ever going to get out of here.'

I translated what she said, but she waved me aside and pulled Kayode closer. Determined to take the conversation into her own hands, she looked him in the eye and spoke directly to him in her heavy English.

'Home or no home?'

Kayode took a step towards the door. He'd finally succeeded in freeing his arm from her grip, and as he turned the handle and stepped out into the corridor, the smile disappeared from his face. 'No home,' he snapped.

I didn't wait to see her reaction; a short sharp shock might anyhow be kinder than keeping her waiting on false pretences. Without glancing back, I followed Kayode, who was now striding towards the stairs. There were heaps of children on the tiled floor, and we didn't see the teenagers we'd passed earlier, or perhaps in our hurry we didn't notice them. The porter was still nowhere to be seen, and we didn't bother looking. Kayode pushed open the door, and as we left the building a gentle breeze licked at our faces, refreshing us after the nausea of being inside.

'Why did you say that?' I asked angrily. 'Because she insulted you? Couldn't we just have cancelled the visit?'

'No, we couldn't,' he said with his habitual smile back in place. 'We had a job to do. Don't think I didn't understand she called me a slave. I'm from Nigeria, my friend. I know what 'abd means. We have Abdullahs and Abdulrahmans too. But I'm a Christian, and Christians forgive.'

'But in some Arabic dialects the word 'abd just means a black person,' I ventured, trying to make out it wasn't as bad as he thought. 'It's not a slur. Anyway, the woman's barely literate.' My voice faltered.

It was obvious I hadn't convinced Kayode, who was no longer smiling. 'That's meant to make it better?' he snorted. 'The word for "black person" is "slave"? Doesn't that just mean the whole language is polluted by hatred? Whatever, I don't have a choice about who I am. I'm black. And being black means either being a Christian or going to prison. Christianity is unique. It makes a virtue out of putting up with humiliation. How else do you explain the fact that half of Africa converted to Christianity in less than a century the moment the first white man arrived? It's not because Christianity was imposed upon us. It's because we needed some way to ennoble the humiliation.'

'You said an hour ago that all Muslims are black. Does that mean all Muslims are Christian too?'

'Precisely. Every Muslim is a black Christian who's strayed from the path, or rather, every Christian is a black Muslim who has succeeded in accepting the shame of their own existence.'

I could see Kayode was about to start on another social theory that played fast and loose with the agreed-upon definitions of common words, but I wasn't in the mood. 'Why did you tell her she didn't have a chance?' I interrupted.

'Because it's true. Her assessment score was extremely low. She has the memory of a goldfish. She lacks the basic mental capacities required to understand her material and temporal surroundings.'

'That's not true at all, Kayode, and you know it. She has a very sharp memory, and she's wiser and more eloquent than the two of us put together. But that test isn't designed for people like her. She comes from the mountains. People in the mountains don't wear watches, and they've never heard of kangaroos.'

'I understand. But unfortunately my job is not to philosophize. Who knows, I might do rather well if it were. My job is to carry out the NHS assessment, and the fact the assessment is flawed or inappropriate doesn't change the truth.'

'The truth?' Kayode was getting on my nerves, and I was raising my voice now. 'What are you talking about?'

'The truth is whatever the assessment score says, and whatever the NHS decides. It's whatever's written in the signed doctors' reports that are saved on the system. The truth is what will determine whether or not she qualifies for independent accommodation. I don't need you to tell me truth is relative, or that truth means one thing for people in the mountains and another thing for you and me. I'm perfectly aware of that. But we're in London, not in the mountains, and we only have one truth. It's not an ideal situation, but societies have to find ways to distinguish between good and bad, acceptable and unacceptable, black and white and so forth. It doesn't matter if the benchmark is wrong. It just has to be agreed upon.'

'Come on, do you really think that woman lacks basic mental capacities?'

'What I think, or for that matter what you think, is irrelevant, and that's how it should be. Because if it were up to me, she'd be out on the street after speaking to me like that, and she'd stay there till she starved to death. These tests might be stupid, but at least they're objective. They eliminate human cruelty. Believe me, the system protects us from ourselves.'

I had a lot to say to Kayode. I could have exploded and told him his theories were a heap of nonsense. I could've told him tests were humanity's most evil invention, all tests, not just the assessments he conducted, because they taught humans to be cruel. I thought of the grim look on my teachers' faces as they handed out the 'fail' marks to the tiny, fragile souls in their care without a grain of pity, or of the pupils who'd passed jumping for joy without noticing their crestfallen classmates who'd failed. Worse, the conviction these tests sow in people's minds, as the school years go by, that people come in 'grades' and 'sets', that people are what their marks say they are, that life is one long test and that those at the top of the class are entitled to feel proud while the failures ought to despise themselves, or at best feel constantly guilty. This, or something like it, is what I should have said to Kayode, even though we both knew there was nothing he or I could do to change the system. Because there was a difference – infinitesimal, to be sure – between wholeheartedly endorsing the sickening state the world was in, and living in it reluctantly. But in the end, I said nothing, because we'd reached a crossroads and needed to go our separate ways. Kayode was turning left, down the high street, to go for lunch at one of its many Turkish restaurants. Actually, he invited me along so we could continue our conversation, but there was a packed lunch I'd made last night waiting for me in the office fridge, and although tuna salad was hardly an inviting prospect, lunch at even a cheap restaurant would set me back ten pounds, which just went to show how life's most minor inconveniences could stand in the way of a person saying great things, or more precisely, how one hundred and fifty grams of tinned fish was all it took to sidetrack my defence of a person who was about to lose their life.

4

Before the day my grandfather left home, never to return, my grandmother Badia didn't tell stories. She says she was timid and as silent as a stone. But when he didn't come back, she couldn't just keep on crying, so she began to invent stories. With no other way to support four girls without a father, she took to knocking on doors in the village to offer her wares. She'd glean a reward for her efforts at each house – a round of bread here, a scoop of dripping there – while the women of the family hovered eagerly around her. Sometimes they'd offer her a cup of tea or a smoke. There was quite a market for her stories; after all, which of the other women in the province, or men for that matter, saw the things she saw?

Every few weeks, officials from the regional police station or sometimes even the governor's office would arrive at her doorstep and take her to town, where they would show her a collection of dead bodies, or what was left of them, flipping them over a few times – naked – for good measure. They instructed her to examine the bodies carefully and indicate if any of them was her husband. When she said no, which she always did, they told her to uncover her eyes and take another look, because death changes a person. When she said no for the second time, they'd send her home to her daughters, and so she'd arrive with a new story or two. A story, say, about a man whose brothers strangled him and threw him in the river so they could get their hands on his inheritance, or about a wife who took revenge on her cheating husband by setting him on fire, leaving nothing but a blistered head buried in a field. Often the stories were about vendettas and honour, but when she was feeling cheerful she'd tell more innocent tales, of seafarers being shipwrecked by sirens' calls or otherwise tricked and tempted by jinns. Her neighbours always awaited her return with great anticipation. For whatever reason, people preferred stories of the dead to the lives of the living; listeners would weep over the deaths of characters they didn't know, filled with a sense of warmth and reverence. Her tales were entirely invented and full of far-fetched exaggerations, and the neighbours loved this too. They were glad to be distracted from the familiar, and adored anything strange and fantastical. Having heard of her remarkable intuition – which she felt was a gift, and those around her seemed to agree – people in the neighbouring villages sometimes sent for her to scrutinize the faces of their dead in cases where there was some suspicion around the circumstances of their demise. She never hesitated. She had a certain notion, which was self-evident to her but in fact was rather unusual. This notion was that a person does not truly die, and their soul does not come to rest, until their body has been seen and their loved ones have satisfied themselves as to how they died. For corpses bear signs which reveal their owner's secrets, at least to those who know how to read them; this skill could only be acquired through practice and long experience, and in matters of death she had more of these than anyone else around.

But for all this, my grandmother would disappoint and irritate the neighbours by rounding off every story with a well-worn maxim, the same one each time, that offered little by way of wisdom. Did all those exciting stories, full of outlandish happenings, really have to end on a note so dull as 'To bury the dead is to honour the dead'? Was that the moral the listener was meant to take from them? Were such wild adventures only there to be tamed and turned into something mundane and ordinary?

To bury the dead is to honour the dead. Those were her parting words as she set off home.

It was a visit from Grandmother Badia in my dreams that persuaded me to take responsibility, even though Ayman had let me off the hook. That night, I waited so long for him to call about the power of attorney and the funeral arrangements that I was worried I'd fall asleep and miss him. I tried to call him several times, but the line went dead after a few rings. I was a bit worried, and messaged him asking to let me know he was OK, but I was also relieved I'd managed to wriggle out of the task for at least another day, and feeling more relaxed, I started getting ready for bed. It was then, around midnight, that my phone rang.

I could have foreseen that things might not go according to plan. Perhaps the embassy's promises to arrange the power of attorney on the same day were over-optimistic and it would take a few days more, or perhaps the parents would change their mind and decide to bring their son's body to Cairo to be buried after all?

But Ayman's voice suggested it was something more serious. He was breathing heavily, his voice coming in and out. I thought he was walking down the street at first, then realized he was standing on his balcony or perhaps at a window that looked out over the street. In the background I could hear the late-night Cairo street sounds you could hear from any balcony in the city. Unmistakable to the trained ear, this after-midnight hubbub drifted up from far below, mixed with a warm, dusty smell and a faint lick of humidity. A jolt of nostalgia went through me; that indefinable soundscape and the sense of company it offered had become the only thing I missed about Cairo, if only barely, and that still tied me to my past in the city. My nostalgic reverie was interrupted by Ayman's swearing, the angry jangle in his voice reminding me that nothing I'd left behind was worth regretting. If there was nothing to regret, then there was certainly nothing to miss.

'This shitty country. This shitty world. I don't know what a person's supposed to do. They wouldn't let them see the kid before he gets buried over there, and they wouldn't even let them hold a funeral here. It's so unfair!'

Ayman had rented out the reception hall of a local mosque, like he'd promised Ghiyath's family he would. He'd tried to find a youth club or similar first because that's what they'd said they'd prefer, but everything was booked up. He thought they were pretty lucky to find a mosque hall available that same day. The attendant had implied he was doing Ayman a big favour as he reproached him for not having reserved further in advance, which Ayman thought was ridiculous; how were a dead person's family meant to know the date of the funeral in advance? Abu Ghiyath had then called some acquaintances in Cairo, mostly fellow Syrians, and invited them to his son's funeral reception. They didn't expect many to come; twenty at most. And yet, though it would be a humble occasion, there was a flicker of energy, even pride, in the man's grief-stricken voice as he told the person on the end of the line that everything would be done according to custom. Ayman could hear approving responses uttered in dignified tones; having been forced to abandon everything, propriety was all they had left.

Umm Ghiyath, meanwhile, was refusing to have anything to do with the reception and instead stayed home with the children. She couldn't shake the notion that the boy wasn't really dead, or had faked it somehow. She also reproached her husband for his unseemly enthusiasm; it wasn't right to hold a funeral when the body was far away in some wintry foreign country. It wasn't the done thing. The whole matter pained her, and she sighed that funerals weren't a quiet affair any more; death these days was every bit as complicated as life itself. Her objections only made Abu Ghiyath more determined to carry out his plans for the reception. It was clear that this funeral, or rather his sense of doing things properly, was filling him with a strange sense of life and restoring his connection to an increasingly distant and shattered past.

When the police turned up at the hall a few minutes after the first funeralgoers arrived, it was clear they didn't share Abu Ghiyath's view. The mosque attendant had decided something was up when he heard the Syrian accents, and immediately reported a suspicious gathering that claimed to be a funeral even though there was no body to be seen. At the time, everything was cause for suspicion, and the TV repeatedly warned citizens to remain alert – especially about foreigners, as usual.

Two plain-clothes officers entered the hall, shook Abu Ghiyath's hand rather coldly and sat down for quarter of an hour, most likely to avail themselves of some coffee. Abu Ghiyath was pleased to see two strangers at the reception, reflecting to himself that it was touching how death brought people together. He too had walked in the funeral processions of people he didn't know, and it had brought him a sense of contentment.

When the two men had finished their coffee, which they relished more than was called for, they asked him to follow them outside. Ayman hurried after them and tried to intervene, but it was too late: Abu Ghiyath's residency permit had expired, and that was all the excuse they needed to arrest him. The reception quickly became an ambush: guests were met by a police van as they left the hall, and nineteen of them spent the night in detention, only a handful having managed to enjoy a cup of coffee first. Just one of Abu Ghiyath's acquaintances, who'd planned to come but luckily got held up on the way, was spared arrest. When he finally arrived at the venue, the police van had left. (This was the sort of serendipitous detail that always caught my attention, and I wished Ayman would tell me a little more, but now wasn't the time.) Umm Ghiyath and the children were later picked up at their flat and brought to the station in a police car. This wouldn't have been so bad had the policeman not insisted on handcuffing her, despite her pleas not to do it in front of the children.

Ayman called a lawyer he knew, who promised to come and help but then failed to show up and turned off his phone. At the police station, the two detectives who'd been assigned the case were not remotely convinced by the excuses as to why there was no coffin or shroud at a funeral, and the parts about London and the embassy only made them more suspicious. They questioned the detainees repeatedly about their relationship to the Muslim Brotherhood, what they thought of President Morsi and the war in Syria, and their views on Hillary Clinton. One of the questions was about Serbia, and this especially alarmed the funeralgoers because they had no idea what sort of opinion they were meant to hold about Serbia or why it could conceivably be of interest to the two policemen. Their hesitation at this particular question was irrefutable proof to the policemen that the suspicious gathering was some sort of political meeting. One of them came to the conclusion –very perspicaciously, he thought – that it was somehow related to the sit-in at Rab'a Square.

At this point, the interrogation took a surprising turn. The less cheerful of the pair turned to Abu Ghiyath and complimented him on the coffee served at the reception, and asked if they'd used a special Syrian recipe to spice the ground beans. Despite the gravity of the situation, Abu Ghiyath almost burst out laughing, and replied awkwardly that it was the mosque attendant who'd ordered the coffee, and that there was nothing Syrian about it. The detective ignored this disappointing answer and continued to wax lyrical about Syrian coffee, which was excellent, as were Syrian kebabs and Syrian sweets, especially Syrian sweets – now *they* were superb. He thought it was witty to joke how grateful he was for the war that had brought all these Syrians and their sweets to Egypt. 'Can't complain!' he chuckled. 'One nation's loss is another's gain.'

The man's boorishness infuriated Ayman, and he almost interrupted. But he had to admit there was some logic to what he was saying, and in any case everyone was laughing along, the grim atmosphere easing slightly. Abu Ghiyath thought this was a good moment to make his *coup de grâce*, risky as it was.

'You know, sir,' he said, 'we're actually Ismailis.'

Big mistake. The other detective twitched like he'd seen a ghost. Practically shaking, he asked Abu Ghiyath to repeat what he'd just said. He obviously hadn't understood, but a cop hunch told him something was up. A person's greatest enemy is always that which they do not know, especially for policemen.

The man had begun to thump the desk in front of him, and the bereaved father was only spared his fury by the intervention of the detective who liked Syrian sweets, and who appeared to be the better educated of the two.

'Ismailis, eh? As in the Assassins and the Aga Khan and all that.'

This settled it for the angry detective. 'If that's what you are, then what are you doing sullying our mosque?' he cried.

There was a deafening silence. Not all of the funeralgoers were Ismaili, but they all kept their mouths shut as they mentally weighed up the danger they were in. Finally one made up his mind. 'Well, *we're* actually Sunnis, detective, honest,' said the man, trying to curry favour by speaking in Egyptian dialect.

One by one, other funeralgoers did the same, in the hope of distancing themselves from Abu Ghiyath. But having only been in Egypt a short while, the poor things hadn't got the hang of how matters worked. There was no point at all opening one's mouth in situations like this; words were traps for those who uttered them (although silence could be equally perilous). The policemen were jubilant; this was what they'd been waiting for since the very beginning of the interrogation, and now it had been handed to them on a platter.

They divided the detained funeralgoers into three groups and began writing up charge sheets. The first group, all Sunnis, were charged with membership of a banned organization, and the second, the Ismailis, with blasphemy and unauthorized assembly. A third group had kept quiet hoping it might save them, or perhaps because they knew it wouldn't make any difference, so to be safe the detective planted a quantity of hashish on each of them, because who knew what they might turn out to be.

The detective who liked sweets concluded the interrogation with an apology. 'Honestly, gentlemen, you're like brothers to us,' he said sincerely, 'but you know how things are these days. We have to take precautions. Ever so sorry.'

The detainees nodded sympathetically, equally sincere in their acceptance of his apology. 'God bless the work you do, sir,' volunteered one.

*

Ayman's voice was heavy with shame as he told me all this. Not only had he let down his guests, who'd come to his home and his country seeking refuge, he'd got them into an even worse mess. He told me I didn't need to arrange the burial any more. The power of attorney hadn't come through, and the whole family were in prison now anyway. Burying the dead was hardly going to make much difference when that was the state the living were in. I even wondered if to hold a funeral in such circumstances might be to make light of the sufferings of those who hadn't died; it was really the living and not the dead who deserved to have ceremonies held in their honour. And yet Ayman implied that he was somehow still expecting something from me. His exact words were 'It's up to you.' What was up to me? I didn't understand. I pretended to agree, and promised I'd let him know the next day if there was anything I could do, and went to bed resolving to forget about the whole thing. It was a pack of nonsense from start to finish – the friendly dolphin, the British embassy, and now the coffee and the Aga Khan and Syrian baklava – and frankly I didn't see what it had to do with me.

Christ's words went round in my head as I drifted off to sleep: 'Let the dead bury their dead.' The phrase was meaningless in the present circumstances, but it felt apt; repeating it to myself in sombre tones, I felt soothed, and reassured that the best course of action was simply to ignore the whole affair.

Grandmother Badia appeared in my dream that night. It was one of those dreams where people don't look or

SHADY LEWIS

sound like they do in real life and yet you know it's them without giving a thought to the strange ease with which names and feelings with long and intimate histories get jumbled up and reassigned to new owners.

My grandmother appeared as Service User A, with a voice similar to hers yet rougher and more confident. I was in her room at the homeless hostel where I'd visited her that morning. Kayode wasn't there; we were alone. For some reason, we were both barefoot, which made me feel awkward and naked. She dragged me by the hand out of the room and began walking purposefully down the long ground-floor corridor. It was dark, but we had no trouble seeing; it also seemed like the people around us couldn't see us even though we could see them. She was speaking to me in a language I didn't understand, which I assumed was Kurdish, and yet I understood everything. As we made our way past the piles of children on the floor she paused and whispered to me: 'Everyone born here is born dead.'

'But these ones aren't dead, Grandmother!' I protested.

She gave me a withering look. 'We're in a dream, pet.'

As I tried to work out the significance of that, Badia pulled me by the hand into the room of the pregnant woman I'd glimpsed that morning sticking her head out of the window. It was still hot and stuffy, and the woman was lying on her back, asleep. From the way her chest rose and fell, it was clear she was struggling to breathe. My grandmother examined her swollen face and gaping mouth for a few seconds, then stroked her thick hair and began to tell me the story of how she'd ended up at the hostel and

78

died a terrible death. As usual, the story was far-fetched, contradictory and full of exaggerations.

'But Grandmother,' I interrupted, 'she's not dead!'

'That doesn't matter,' she snapped. 'She'll die at some point, won't she?'

I had the feeling she was trying to make me feel guilty for some reason, and resisted as best I could. There was nothing I could do for the people here, or anywhere else, and the feeling of helplessness was already enough. I didn't need a guilty conscience on top.

'Sweetheart, this is a dream. Try to help her in the dream at least!'

'Help her? Me? The only thing I've ever achieved was leaving the country.'

'So you think you got away, do you?'

I tried to open the window but couldn't, and only succeeded in making a loud noise that I worried would wake the woman. I gave up almost immediately, as usual. Meanwhile, my grandmother was on a mission and continued to drag me from room to room, where everyone was asleep or half-dead. She came up with a tragic story to match each person, and it was clear from her breaking voice that she wasn't finding it easy, despite her long experience. The stories weren't just set nearby, in London and Liverpool and Belfast, but also far away, in all the places these people had come from: Pakistan, Nigeria, India, Bolivia, Algeria, Bulgaria, South Africa, Trinidad – every patch of earth you could imagine. I was amazed my grandmother even knew the names of these countries.

I was beginning to feel tired, and she noticed. She led

me out of the building; we were still barefoot, and I was nervous someone would notice us, but out on the street an explosion of bright coloured lights and a joyful clamour mixed with loud music distracted me. Everything was different outside, and I felt like we'd entered another world altogether.

It was in the small hours, perhaps close to dawn, and the street was packed. Groups of drunken young people staggered from bar to bar, laughing lustily, and lovers walked entwined in each other's arms, clinging on tightly so the force of their joy wouldn't knock them to the ground. It looked more like a huge, good-natured riot than the usual rowdy London Saturday night. Everyone was happy and wild.

A passer-by stopped a few metres from us, legless by the looks of it, and leaned against the building with one hand. With the other hand, he fumbled with his fly, took out his dick and urinated right next to the entrance, letting out a long, wavering groan like he was orgasming. I thought he hadn't noticed us, but as soon as he'd done up his fly he turned to us, smiled broadly, then bounded over with surprising grace. 'Evening, mate!' he cried, throwing his arm around my neck. 'Evening all!'

Feeling genuinely happy, I waved goodbye as he went on his way. I wanted to stop him and tell him how lucky he was that he knew nothing about this building, which contained all the world's sorrows – literally all of them, or specimens of each one at least. The idea occurred to me that perhaps the hostel was a trap designed to soak up all earthly misery and its miserable victims and hide them away from outsiders so as not to disturb their peace of mind by day or their merrymaking by night, and that that was why it had to remain a secret known only to a handful of people.

Having forgotten about my grandmother for a moment, I quickly looked around for her. She was still standing behind me, but she looked different now, like herself, and I sensed that this meant the dream was coming to an end. 'Go,' she said. 'Get away from here.'

I tried to run, but my muscles froze, like they do in nightmares, and I didn't know what direction to go in or what exactly I was running from. 'I don't know the way, Grandmother,' I panted, 'and my phone's dead!'

'I've told you a hundred times to charge your phone before you go to bed!'

With that I jerked awake, my eyes already half-open and one hand flailing at the bedside table. When my fingers finally found my phone, I was relieved to find it plugged in, but any sense of relief melted away the second I looked at the screen. There were eighteen missed calls from Kayode, most of them in the early hours. We did not have the kind of relationship where we could call each other at four in the morning. It struck me that I didn't have anyone in London I knew well enough to call at four in the morning. The thought made me sad; if you don't have friends you can call at four in the morning, then essentially you don't have friends. But I quickly regained my focus and opened the message Kayode had sent at five.

Call me when you get this it's vv important.

Kayode couldn't have slept at all, because there was another from a quarter to six: *Pls don't go to office or*

81

speak to ppl from work before we have talked. Need to discuss sth important.

As I was rereading the message, my phone began to buzz in my hand. Kayode again. He'd got me worried, but I was so annoyed by his persistence I decided not to pick up. I got it: he wanted to talk to me. There was no need for all this. I jabbed at the red button to decline the call. Within a few seconds, I'd resolved not to go to work. I preferred to ignore problems, and there was clearly a problem here. I composed a short message to my boss claiming to be ill and requesting the day off, then went into my Messenger inbox to search my conversation with Ayman for the address of the hospital where Ghiyath's body had been taken. My grandmother's night-time visit had persuaded me that if I couldn't be any use to the living, the least I could do was try to help the dead.

I didn't want to waste time, so I jumped out of bed and within a few minutes was walking to the Tube. I'd put on a shirt I only wore for important occasions. I normally went to the office in a T-shirt – it would be humiliating to dress up for such a low-ranking job – and since I was rarely invited to anything that required me to dress smartly, it was three years since I'd last worn a shirt. That was when I'd gone to swear the Oath of allegiance to the Queen in order to get citizenship. I didn't meet the Queen, of course, but I stood in front of a photo of her, talking at it like a crazy person. Thinking about this also made me sad. What fun was life if you only got the chance to wear a shirt once every few years? How often you got dressed up said a lot about you and how far you'd come in life.

When I arrived, I cheered up, because the journey had been so quick – three stops on the Tube. I liked Whitechapel and felt more at home there than anywhere else in London. It was full of contradictions that always made me chuckle. Despite the name, for example, its principal landmark was a large white mosque, and most of the people who lived there were Muslim. There was also Brick Lane, famed for its Indian restaurants, but as everyone knew, pretty much all of these were Bangladeshi rather than Indian. It was this sort of thing, which I discovered early on, that trained me to doubt much of what I encountered in London, and treat the relationships between names and their objects with a healthy scepticism.

In the few minutes it took me to cross the road from the station to the hospital, I was filled with the joyful thoughts that greeted me whenever I came to Whitechapel. How accommodating the English and their language were! They were as indulgent with signifiers and meanings as they were with everything else, especially when India was involved in some way. I'm not talking about the East India Company and whether or not it was actually a company, or how companies transform themselves into empires, or empires into companies, as they do these days; I mean things that have nothing to do with India at all. Like Caribbean islands being referred to as the 'West Indies', or Indigenous Americans as 'Red Indians', or like a Scottish linguist deciding that a chunk of the world should be known by the fanciful term 'Indo-China'. I could never decide whether names like this were evidence of a wild, unbridled imagination or an extreme, humourless parochialism. The funniest thing was that 'Indo-China' had stuck. No wonder, then, when the English language had done such a number on world geography, that the white mosque should become Whitechapel or indeed Greenchapel, that the UK should be renowned for its tea or that Indian khichri should end up as kushari, the pride of Egypt's proletarian cuisine. It flashed momentarily through my head that Kayode had got it all wrong. We weren't all black, as he would have it. No, we were all Indian!

But I couldn't follow this train of thought any further, because just as I was ruminating on kushari, a hospital receptionist asked me the purpose of my visit. Oddly, I was unprepared. What was I meant to say? That I was there to pick up the corpse of someone I didn't know? To conceal my confusion, I took out my work ID and thrust it towards him, deciding to pretend I was there in an official capacity. 'I'm here about a body.'

It worked even better than I'd expected. With a curt nod, the receptionist said, 'Fourth floor. Room 415.' It was that easy.

Finding the office, however, was going to require my full attention. One of the four lifts was out of service, and there was a crowd of patients and visitors congregating in front of them, so I took the stairs. The hospital corridors were labyrinthine, reminding me of the huge, multistorey homeless shelters I regularly visited for work, but I didn't pause to consider this resemblance any further and instead focused on the room numbers. Twice I ended up back where I'd started before finally spotting 415 to my right.

The door was ajar. I knocked before peering inside. There was nobody there, and it was exceedingly small, with only enough space for a half-size desk and chair where your face would probably touch the computer screen if you tried to sit down. I felt sorry for whoever had to work there.

Suddenly, I heard a friendly voice behind me: 'Hello there, can I help you?'

I withdrew my head and turned around to see a tall, skinny man with a prominent Adam's apple, looking very surprised to see me.

'I've come about a body,' I replied. 'To make arrangements for the burial.'

'Well, you're in the right place then,' said the man. 'Are you Egyptian?'

'Er, yes… How did you know?'

'Oh, you look very Egyptian. Straight out of the British Museum!'

'I see. So who's the person I need to speak to?'

'I'm a big fan of Ancient Egypt. I was obsessed when I was at school.'

'Great. Um, do you think you could answer my question?'

'Of course, I'm the person you need to speak to! Now tell me, have you visited the Pyramids?'

'Not much, no, but could we—'

'Really? How come?'

'I don't know, it's just not a thing in Egypt. Anyway, I'm looking for someone who died on Monday.'

'But you are Egyptian?'

85

'Yes.'

'And you haven't visited the Pyramids very much?'

'Correct.'

'That's the strangest thing I've ever heard. How many times have you been?'

'Once, maybe twice. So, the man I'm looking for was Syrian.'

'Well there you go. I'm from New Zealand, and I originally came here to join an orchestra. I play the double bass – you know, the big one.'

'How interesting. Do you know anything about the body? Name was Ghiyath?'

'Of course, bear with me. You see, I didn't get the orchestra job in the end—'

'I'm sorry to hear it. He was around twenty.'

'Ah! He looked much younger. So anyway, I ended up with the cotton man job here. Not something I imagined I'd be doing, I must say.'

'Cotton man?'

'That's the one. Right at the very end, the body comes to me and I give it the once-over before we pass it on for burial. The orifices are all stuffed with cotton, and men get their bits tied up with some thread. That's my job.'

'What for?'

'To stop any liquids from leaking out. Otherwise it looks pretty gruesome. Your friend arrived in a real state. He must have been dead for a while. His clothes were soaked in urine and faeces and his face was covered in blood and snot.'

'So what did you do about that?'

'Oh, don't worry, I took care of it. I'm not going to lie though, it wasn't easy. If I could give you one piece of advice, it would be not to die like he did. Make sure they find you within half a day. Tops. Or put it this way – live alone if you want to, but when you die, make sure you have people around you.'

'Well, it sounds like a tough job… is it possible to see the body?'

'It certainly is tough. I used to hate it. But then I started to like it. And it's a very Egyptian job. As Egyptian as those pharaonic features of yours.'

'Excuse me?'

'Think about it – mummification and all that. I'm the mummifier. The last one to touch the body, the one who prepares it for the next life. I know a lot about Egypt, you know.'

'So I see.'

'You might not think it's an important job, but it lies at the heart of human dignity. And people never stop to think about dignity until they encounter death.'

'Exactly. That's why I'm here. And I need you to help me.'

'Just one last question.'

'Sure.'

'You know the crown Horus wore? The white crown of Upper Egypt?'

'Vaguely.'

'You know how it looks like a bowling pin?'

'I suppose, yeah?'

'Funny, isn't it. Do you know how that came about?'

My patience was wearing thin. How the hell was I sup-posed to know why Horus's crown looked like a skittle? This moron seemed to think I'd crawled out of a Pharaoh's tomb and travelled to London on a solar barque. I was just a piece of the scenery in whatever trip he was on. To him, the place I came from existed somewhere five thousand years in the past. I was about to snap when the person whose office it was appeared, interrupting our conversation, and asked him to leave in a brusque tone I couldn't read. He didn't respond, but shuffled a few steps out of the way and stood in the corridor looking back at her defiantly. There wasn't space in the office for the two of us, so I remained standing outside while we talked, which took two minutes at the most. When I told her why I was there, she asked me if I had any proof I was a relation, or a power of attorney from the family. When I started to explain that the situa-tion was complicated, she cut me off, asked me to leave, and closed the door.

So that was it. I had done all I could.

5

Nayil, my maternal cousin, was seven whole years older than me. The first grandchild of my Grandmother Badia, he was the occasion for many of her stories, as well as a good quantity of her tears. As the saying goes, the only thing more beloved than a son is a grandson.

His mother was my Aunt Hilana, Badia's firstborn and the most hard done by of the four sisters. She'd never gone to school or learned to read and write, and instead had had twelve sons, most of whose names I didn't know; the eldest hadn't attended school either, while the youngest had a PhD. The thing was that Hilana, despite being officially uneducated, was in reality a highly cultured woman by virtue of listening to the radio twenty-four hours a day. She didn't even turn the volume down when she went to bed. She listened almost exclusively to the BBC, though in autumn she sometimes tuned in to Radio Monte Carlo; she herself had no explanation for these seasonal preferences. Hilana was not merely a loyal listener but had strong opinions on international politics (and everything else besides), which she expressed very forcefully. For example, she was still of the view that it had been a grave mistake to accept China into the international community, and would declaim phrases such as 'The Formosa government is the sole legitimate representative of the Chinese people.' When a foolhardy relative once pointed out that it wasn't called Formosa any more, she hit the roof. One threatening finger raised, she launched into a long tirade about Peking's defiance of the international order. 'Formosa!' she thundered, 'not Taiwan! And not Macao!'

This was just one of the scenes to which the villagers were regularly treated, and they enjoyed them as much as Grandmother Badia's stories. The pair made a sensational double act: Grandmother was a countrywoman through and through, and talked like the women from rural Upper Egypt, while Hilana sounded like a Yorkshire gent who'd studied at Oxford and voted Tory like his father and grandfather before him. My aunt never hid her neoliberal leanings; she thought Thatcher was the greatest politician the world had produced. The reason she gave for this was the strangest part of the whole thing. *Sitt Mergret*, as she grandly referred to her, had invented a kind of ice cream that could be produced in small, portable machines, thus helping shopkeepers become more competitive and self-sufficient (to my surprise, I later found out there was some truth to this story). Being a woman of action, Hilana purchased one of the ice-cream machines she claimed Thatcher had invented, set it up outside her house and proceeded to sell ice cream to the neighbours' children. It was a highly profitable concern until local shopkeepers began to buy their own machines, which became known as Mergretas, and Hilana's business dried up. She nevertheless remained the most fervent Thatcherite in Upper Egypt and perhaps the whole country, supporting her staunchly on the right to buy, pit closures and the Falklands. This was in sharp distinction to her mother, who owned a Chinese-made stove and sided with Argentina in the conflict. Badia felt a deep solidarity with Latin America; every other month, she'd buy cheap frozen Brazilian beef from the food cooperative, reasoning that 'Good people don't abandon old friends.' She didn't have strong feelings about the British themselves, but she harboured a special rancour towards their livestock. She always used to say that during the war the British had requisitioned the peasants' harvests to feed their horses, and many people had starved to death. She never specified which one, but we knew she meant the First World War.

Perhaps it was because of these ideological differences that my grandmother and aunt's accounts of Nayil's death focused on such different aspects of what had happened. Like his grandfather, my cousin left one day and never came back. His body was never found. My grandmother said either he'd been swallowed up by the desert, or he'd lost his mind when he heard the bombs and saw the dead bodies, and had wandered off and been eaten by beasts. Hilana maintained that he'd died leaping in front of his comrades to save them from artillery fire, and been so blown to pieces there was nothing left to be gathered up. Grandmother's version focused on the tragedy of his death, alone in Hafr al-Batin, whereas Aunt Hilana, being a small-business owner, was more concerned with notions of duty, the international consensus on the war to liberate Kuwait, and most importantly the compensation payment she was due from the army, which was a considerable sum in those days and compared favourably with the price of a boy on the open market.

None of these things were of interest to me; indeed nobody back then was bothered by the fate of the eighteen-year-old boy who'd been shipped off to hell. Everyone was distracted by Egypt's debt being written off, or half of it at least, and busy listening to a sorrowful Kuwaiti song called 'God We Do Not Oppose Your Will', which was actually pretty good. But there was an episode in Grandmother's stories about Nayil and his adventures in the desert that did appeal to me, one she recounted over and over. The boy's camp was next to a US camp (the cousins of the British, as my aunt used to declare to our amusement). In this US camp there were also female soldiers, pretty and blonde and sweet, with camouflage uniforms and guns. At night, they would sneak into the camp next door looking for Nayil, and when they found him they'd shower him with hugs and kisses and gifts. This made his comrades extremely jealous, naturally. It was no mystery why they did this, because between kisses the blonde soldiers would say, 'You're a Christian, here's a biscuit!' Then they'd throw their arms affectionately around him. 'You're a Christian, here's some milk! Here's some chocolate!'

I always found this hilarious, and indeed anyone who heard Grandmother's American accent couldn't help but laugh. She'd pronounce the word for Christian, *masihi*, just the way they did, *moosihi*, with the *h* sound all wrong, and when we laughed she'd exaggerate even more, twisting her tongue helplessly around the words in theatrical imitation of the blonde soldiers' flirtatious broken Arabic. Badia's performance wasn't terribly convincing, but as a child I was impressionable enough to believe that if the Americans, or even their cousins the British, ever set eyes on me, they would sweep me up in their embrace. For years, I dreamed of the day I'd travel to the land of biscuits and chocolate, or the day the blonde women would come to visit us in Egypt.

The best thing of all about Grandmother's stories were that they were so contradictory, new parts abrogating old – or at least coexisting with them – without her feeling any need to apologize or explain. This is a classic feature of prolific storytellers and overactive imaginations. When Uncle Tanios crossed the sea to Italy, Grandmother became rather xenophobic. In the version she told of his story, when his vessel approached the coast everyone aboard threw themselves into the waves and swam for shore. Tanios had taken nothing with him but a gilded wooden icon of Mary Mother of Light, to watch over him and keep him safe from harm on his journey. However, the icon would perform other functions too. When my uncle washed up on the beach near a small seaside town, where he knew no one and spoke not a word of the language, the Virgin was to be his only means of communication. As soon as he made land, he set off at a run without a backward glance, and within half an hour was in the town square. He approached the first person he saw, and with a broad smile held up the icon with both hands, pointed at her with one finger and then pointed at himself. When he'd tried this a few times and realized it meant nothing to the man, he crossed himself and rolled up one sleeve of his still-wet shirt to reveal the bluish cross tattooed on his wrist and held it up, no longer smiling. Mystified, the Italian pushed Uncle Tanios roughly and somewhat pityingly aside, then carried on his way.

Uncle Tanios did not despair; despair was not an option. He was hungry, wet and close to collapsing. He hurried from one person to another in the main square and repeated the same routine, brandishing the icon above his head as if at a demonstration. None of the Italians had a clue what he was doing, but he was heartened when an older woman began to cross herself along with him and kissed the icon, then handed him some coins, though he didn't know what they were worth or how to spend them. Soon it was night-time, and Uncle Tanios bedded down in the square, exhausted. He placed the icon in front of him. A few passers-by tossed him some change, and a child offered him half a sandwich.

Shortly before midnight, an official-looking car pulled up and took Uncle Tanios to a small church. He was over-joyed when they gave him hot soup and clean clothes and led him to a bedroom. There he saw he would be sharing with a friendly young man from Afghanistan. Uncle Tanios didn't sleep a wink that night, but cried more bitterly than he had ever cried before. They'd put him in a shared room with a Muslim, and treated him like a Muslim. It was the saddest moment of his life.

This part was all Badia knew, but there was more. Many years later, my uncle visited me in London, to see for himself whether I really did have a chair at work. Once my honesty had been established, he opened his heart to me and told me the whole story.

He'd got his first job in Italy at a steelworks, where his colleagues had taken a liking to him and invited him to join something called a book club. They explained to him that the icon he brought to work and clutched throughout the lunch break was not going to do him any favours. The country had far too many icons already, they told him, and people were sick of both icons and their owners; he'd make himself more friends by publicly smashing it to pieces. Uncle Tanios obviously wasn't going to do that, perish the thought; he hadn't survived the perilous trip to Europe only to abandon his faith. But he did put his icon aside, and his co-workers liked that. They taught him to read and write Italian and gave him books. He went for beers with them on Friday evenings, and danced with their girls on Saturday nights. When he got to this point in the story, he lowered his voice. 'They were communists, you see,' he whispered in embarrassment. 'Communists are kind people, and they like foreigners.'

He didn't become a communist and they didn't ask him to, but when there were huge strikes in Milan in the early 1980s, he had to stand by his comrades. His task seemed straightforward, but it was risky: he was to stand at the gates of a factory with a crowbar, and stop scabs getting in. The first day passed without event, but on the second day, the factory owners brought in workers from out of town. Uncle Tanios found that they looked like him; they'd washed up on the beach in boats, like he had. A fight broke out, and Uncle Tanios, who was a vigorous young man back then, saw red and split a man's head open with his crowbar. The man dropped to the ground. When Tanios saw the blood on his hands and clothes, he dropped the crowbar and ran. He told me he'd run for days without stopping, and when he finally stopped to rest and catch his breath, the strike was over. Some of his comrades were in jail, and the communists had vanished from the city and indeed the country. After that, Uncle Tanios found a new job in a restaurant owned by the wife of a famous man called Berlusconi. He had a photo of himself with the couple before they separated, which he treasured.

When I reached this little island, I wasn't as lucky as Nayil had been with the blonde soldiers, or as Tanios had been with the Italian communists. I wasn't expecting a warm reception; Grandmother had warned me that the grandchildren of the people who'd stolen from the poor to feed their animals weren't going to care about icons. Aunt Hilana, meanwhile, told me the communists in the UK had been wiped out when Thatcher invented her ice-cream machine, which everyone bought with easy loans around the same time their Italian comrades had been defeated. Nobody had noticed because they were busy paying off the loans and redecorating their newly purchased council houses.

In the event, I was treated like a Muslim. And there were worse things than being made to share a room with one. I was stopped and searched at airports like a Muslim, had my papers checked as thoroughly as Muslims did, and got asked the same ridiculous questions they asked Muslims. Once, at Heathrow, I told them off the bat that I wasn't

Muslim. They were amazed and uncomprehending. When I went on to say that I was Christian, and that there were a lot of us in Egypt, they became slightly alarmed and warned me not to 'make things more complicated'. I often aroused fear, and that was a heavy cross to bear. Attractive women in bars and on dimly lit side streets would get as nervous around me as they did around Muslims. In the vicinity of schools and playgrounds, parents would fear for their children when they saw me, just like they did with Muslims.

Most people were well intentioned and only denied that I wasn't a Muslim because it disrupted the strict order that governed their world. I couldn't blame them. Generally speaking, a good system of categories, neatly delineated and unambiguously named, is indispensable, and there's no reason why the rules should be bent to suit the one person, like me, who happens to be an exception, or indeed the ten million like me who happen to be exceptions. One simply has to assume good intentions. My neighbour in the flat opposite, for example, always insisted on wishing me a happy Ramadan and Eid Mubarak every year, and always got the dates right. At first, I used to tell him that I wasn't Muslim. He'd drop his voice to a whisper. 'No need to be shy about it,' he'd reply with a wink. 'I won't tell anyone!' Then he'd bid me goodbye with a wave and a cheery 'salam aleikum!' or 'alhamdulillah!'

The attitude at the office was also commendable, attesting to a fairly solid understanding of world religions and a shaky grasp of geography. My colleagues would do a double take, some gasping audibly, when they saw me holding a pint, which was every Friday when we all went to the pub after work. 'We didn't know you drank alcohol!' they'd exclaim. This went on for years, and yet their amazement remained fresh and childlike each time. At work parties, when our boss, a Scotsman, would order pizza for the whole team, he'd always make sure to get one that was halal especially for me, which I'd then ungraciously swap slices of for my colleagues' ham-laden versions. I liked ham, though I didn't eat it often. Time and again, this would leave them reeling in surprise. 'Isn't pork haram?' they'd ask earnestly, while my boss looked on sadly.

But you can achieve a lot by simply wearing a person down. To begin with, I let my stubble go unshaven; beards were in fashion at that point. Then one day I shaved off my moustache by mistake. I stopped going to the pub after work on Fridays to save money, and secretly I was starting to regard it as a little undignified. Soon afterwards I began to have stomach issues, and gave up drinking altogether. For the same reason – and I started getting heartburn too – I became a lot pickier about my food, both halal and haram. When the dentist told me I needed to take better care of my gums, I got into the habit of strolling down the high street with a miswak in hand. I took to wearing an above-the-ankle thobe at the weekends because it was comfier and always got me plenty of attention. After all this, it felt only natural to try fasting at Ramadan; maybe it would help with my stomach issues.

This was much more comfortable for everyone around me, restoring their peace of mind and reinstating the image of the world as it appeared to Border Agency officers. My neighbour was thrilled; the police officers who stop and searched me at train stations were able to do so with a clear conscience; and my boss could get the warm glow of cultural sensitivity every time he ordered me a pizza. People went wild over the shalwar kameez I bought for a Sikh friend's wedding. 'Islamic dress is gorgeous,' sighed one of my colleagues as she gazed in awe at the sparkling embroidery. 'Islam is just so beautiful!'

All these transformations only caused me a new set of problems. For a start, real Muslims never accepted me as one of their own. None of them ever addressed me as 'brother', no matter how hard I tried to prove worthy. Some of them thought I was taking the mickey; this happened especially when I got overexcited and found myself adding 'mashallah' to the end of all my sentences. A couple of them started a nasty campaign against me and went so far as to convince the guys at the chicken shop near my house that selling halal chicken to non-Muslims was haram. That really hurt, because the fried chicken there was very good – crispy on the outside, tender on the inside – and very reasonably priced.

This was probably what was going round in my mind when I lunged at the Cotton Man, grabbed him by the collar and began screaming incomprehensibly in his face. I just couldn't stop myself when I heard him say, proudly and without the least regard for my feelings, 'Salam aleikum.' The guy had followed me all the way out of the hospital, and this was what he had to say?

The look of fear in his eyes as he tried to wrest his collar from my grip returned me to my senses, and I felt instantly embarrassed. People passing us at the hospital gates were staring, probably thinking I was a mental health case, which was fair enough. An apology wouldn't cover it, and I didn't have any justification for my reaction. Spelling it all out would take as much effort as it had taken me to try and describe to a British friend of mine what fenugreek smells like, and would be equally futile.

'It's all – just – getting – too much,' I choked, forcing the words out. 'Too much.'

Of course he had no idea what I was talking about, and he stared at me, waiting for a more satisfactory answer. I was forced to explain that greetings weren't as innocent as they seemed, and that expressions or words that might appear neutral, right down to prepositions, came with their own histories and battles and could be cruel and frightening. This was also unsatisfactory.

'I don't know what you mean,' he burst out, looking upset. 'I was trying to be nice!'

I tried to extricate myself politely, because he was never going to understand anyway.

'It's very complicated,' I intoned as if revealing one of the secrets of the Orient, 'so let me put it like this. As a greeting, it is not appropriate to use "salam aleikum", either with me personally or in this situation.'

But my trick didn't work, because failing to understand this cryptic, profound-sounding response only made him feel mocked. He stepped back, took a deep breath and gazed into the air as if he understood but wasn't convinced. 'That might be so,' he said, one eyebrow raised, 'but it doesn't explain why you're so angry.'

I don't know why I let myself get drawn into explaining everything to that lunatic. Maybe I wanted to prove I wasn't mentally ill; brown people are regularly accused of being impulsive and angry, and so we often find ourselves obliged to justify the mildest signs of anger, sadness, despair, or any other feeling considered undesirable in this country. Although they were highly relevant, I resolved to leave the stories about Nayil and Uncle Tanios out of it, because I didn't want to seem like I was on a personal crusade. Keeping things general, I began at the end of the story.

'Well,' I sighed, 'in our country there used to be a lot of greetings, a wonderful mix of all the different ways you could possibly conceive of to say hello to somebody or wish them well. You'd take the word "morning" and add the name of some kind of flower, rose or jasmine, to make a morning greeting. For the evening, you could add a sweet foodstuff like honey or cream. You could add colours and wish someone a white day or a green day. You could add an abstract noun to the time of day and wish someone, say, a morning of goodness, or an evening of beauty or happiness. Often we'd reference natural phenomena with transcendental associations by wishing people a morning of light, for example, or a dew-laden day, even to the point of contradiction, like with evening of light. Sometimes people would be playful and come up with less common ones, like morning of almond, to which someone would reply "morning of walnut", or even "morning of morning", which is truly genius if you ask me – even more so than using nuts for greetings. All this was an art form which required a person to be trained from a young age. It took skill to compose and deploy these greetings, and to select the appropriate response according to situation, status and other factors.'

The Cotton Man was keeping up better than I'd anticipated. 'So where have all those greetings gone then?' he shot back, looking pleased with his perspicacity.

'Well, I don't know exactly,' I mused. 'It happened gradually. There was a conspiracy against greetings, though I can't say whether the aim was to eliminate them entirely or monopolize them. Some people said it was a waste of time to have so many greetings, and that it had an impact on productivity. Others said it encouraged hypocrisy, because the more people greeted each other, the less well they knew each other. The real hardliners said it was blasphemous, because mornings belonged to God alone, and attributing them to all sorts of other things amounted to polytheism, or encouraged polytheistic attitudes. Vicious attacks came in from all quarters, smearing the reputation of one greeting after another. People began to find them distasteful, making pained faces whenever they heard one. Soon whole generations grew up without hearing the greetings we'd used in the past. One group of people came up with the idea that everyone should use a single greeting, presumably thinking – and rightly so – that if they could control how people said hello to each other when they opened their eyes in the morning, then they could also control their days and nights, their hearts and minds. And duly people were indoctrinated. If anyone greeted them with anything but the standard greeting, they would either ignore the person

until they returned to their senses, or simply respond with
their own greeting in a tone that met the ear like a slap to
the face or a gob of spit in the eye.'

'So it was a war!' exclaimed the Cotton Man. His dis-
play of emotion was exaggerated, and the frown of concern
looked out of place on his twenty-something face, yet he
seemed sincere. 'It's so scary that every single greeting
became a battleground.'

I realized all this background wasn't as difficult to grasp
as I'd imagined. After all, words and expressions had their
own, much fought-over, history here too. And probably
everywhere for that matter.

'Yeah, it was a massacre. They butchered so many
greetings, and so many relationships were ruined – between
neighbours, colleagues, relatives. And the tragic thing is
that a greeting which is made in peace and in the name
of peace has become a battle cry. People were divided
into two camps, one fighting for the "greeting of Islam"
and one rallying under the slogan "Religion belongs to
God and greetings belong to us all". But the civil war of
greetings didn't last long. It was swiftly settled, though it
left festering wounds that have not yet healed. Every time
we're forced to say "salam aleikum" or "aleikum salam",
we relive the bitterness of defeat, because we know we're
saying it under duress, and there's nothing worse than the
gloating looks of the winners as we greet them.'

As I was talking, the Cotton Man had bowed his tall
frame slightly, perhaps in an intentional expression of
sympathy. 'I understand, and I'm so sorry,' he said mourn-
fully, a pitying look in his eyes. 'I didn't mean to bring up

all this trauma for you. Maybe you should try therapy or something?'

The moron! So in the end he hadn't understood anything at all. I was just another brown person with an anger problem who needed to see a doctor. Like we all had some virus that required medical intervention. He didn't get it. I wanted to scream at him that if he'd just said 'hi' like a normal person instead of showing off his ludicrous conversational Arabic, we would have saved ourselves this whole embarrassing situation. But I couldn't raise my voice, because that would only confirm his view. So I went along with him for the sake of farce.

'I did, as it happens, and my therapist told me to listen to this song that goes "*Sabah al-kheir ya dunya*, good morning, bonjour!" every morning when I wake up.' This was a real Egyptian children's song, which I liked, and I did actually hum it to myself on mornings when I felt depressed, but he didn't realize I was pulling his leg and asked me in concerned, compassionate tones if it had worked. So then I couldn't take it back. Of course it's unkind to make fun of someone who doesn't know they're being made fun of, especially when they're well intentioned, but he didn't give me a chance.

'Oh, like magic!' I said after a second's hesitation. 'Honestly, mate, I've come a long way on my journey of healing.'

I almost started singing it to him; there was a catchy bit that went 'Hello world, say it back to me, say *sabah al-nur*!'. But the Cotton Man saved us both the embarrassment. 'Listen,' he interrupted, 'the body will be leaving for burial tomorrow, because they can't keep it here any longer.'

He'd listened to my conversation with the woman in the tiny office, and heard her summarily dismissing me without giving me any information about the body I'd come to ask about, and that was why he'd followed me out of the hospital. He told me all this in a whisper, looking nervously around him. I couldn't work out at first if he was genuinely scared of being seen, or if he thought this performance would make him sound important. When I asked if he was sure, he seemed insulted.

'A hundred per cent!' the Cotton Man shouted, so loudly that a woman in a wheelchair who was on her way out of the gate turned around and shot him an annoyed look. 'There are strict procedures! They had to put these rules in place as soon as refrigerators were first invented – how long you could keep a body in a hospital, when it had to be buried or disposed of. You know, you can keep a dead body in a fridge for ever without it decomposing, and that's a very dangerous thing. People could easily start getting confused about death and immortality, or finding it hard to forget about their dead. It isn't cheap either, and you know all about austerity and the strain it's putting on hospitals. That affects the living and the dead.'

There was a crazed gleam in the Cotton Man's eye as he rambled about the historical role of morgue refrigerators, yet something made me trust him. When I asked him what would happen next, I felt even surer, because his answer was elaborate and convincing. Since no one had claimed the body so far, he said, Social Services would step in, because the job of Social Services was to take care of anyone who couldn't take care of themselves: children, the elderly, the mentally ill, and of course the dead. In doing so they would consider both the needs of the cared-for individual and the public interest, within the parameters of the budget available. Clearly it was in the public interest to bury a body as quickly and as cheaply as possible, but it was impossible to say what the needs of the deceased person were. And so it had to be assumed that the interests of the individual and the public were one and the same. There were only a few Islamic cemeteries nearby, and he'd find out by the end of the day which one the body was destined for, and when, and promised to let me know – provided I kept it to myself. I felt genuinely grateful, and a little guilty.

'Thank you so much,' I said. 'It's really kind of you. And sorry if I was harsh before. I just didn't get the whole Pharaohs thing, you know? It seemed a bit over the top.'

With this apology I tried to leave, but I couldn't get away until we'd agreed how we were going to keep in touch. The Cotton Man suggested we take each other's work numbers; for some reason, he made a thing about not wanting to swap personal numbers, which was fine by me. It was bound to take a few minutes; I'd had my phone off all morning so as to avoid Kayode, but now I'd have to risk turning it on so as to save the mobile number of the refrigerator department. While I was doing that, he seized the opportunity to continue blathering on about the Pharoahs. I wasn't interested in any of it, but I had to admit he made me laugh a few times. The funniest bit was when he asked me if I knew what form the god Ra had taken when he created humans and other earthly creatures. I had no idea; I would have assumed a bull or eagle, say, but there was no way I could have guessed the right answer, which the Cotton Man told me while practically falling over laughing: a goose. He repeated this piece of information several times over, laughing harder every time. He stopped for long enough to comment that the Ancient Egyptians were hilarious, and he was right. It struck me that history as a whole was generally pretty funny, and that its aim was to make us feel better about ourselves and what we had by comparing it with the past. As I was musing on this, he interrupted me to give me his number, so I saved it and gave him mine, and finally it looked like our meeting had come to an end.

'Do you know what the Ancient Egyptians' worst insult was?' he asked, gripping the hand I'd extended to him in farewell. I shrugged impatiently; he wasn't expecting an answer. His features were instantly solemn again as he told me what the ancient papyri had revealed.

'O ye of the empty tomb.'

6

The British are sharp as a tack. They can sell anything. They sold opium to the Chinese, then bought tea, took it to India and sold that to the Indians (and more opium, of course). Tea became British, as did most things. They say they are a nation of shopkeepers, which is not only true but reveals the virtues of both self-deprecation and self-reliance that any good trader must possess. Naturally the British stopped dealing hard drugs once they'd got the world hooked on tea, and on this point my Aunt Hilana was quite right. When her village neighbours made fun of her for so keenly following British politics – 'Fancy yourself English, do you?' – she'd simply raise the cup of black tea that never left her hand and reply, 'Don't we all.' Then she'd point a threatening finger at the tea leaves, and that was enough for them to understand what she meant and bow their heads. Auntie Hilana always used to say that the secret to British success wasn't so much that they'd turned a good profit on tea, but that they taught the world how to enjoy a nice cup of tea and even went to war for the sake of it. A nice cup of tea is an idea, and ideas are the most lucrative business of all.

She certainly knew more about the British than I did, even though I'd lived here for years. I rarely got the chance to meet any of them, and when I did, they were very different to the British people I'd read about in books or seen in films. Some didn't drink tea at all, and they'd never heard of the Opium Wars. Obviously one shouldn't be so naive as to believe everything one reads in books or sees in films, but still, you'd think people would at least try to model their behaviour after the classics of cinema and literature, the British as much as anyone else. But apparently *A Tale of Two Cities*, which was on our high school English curriculum, was slightly out of date.

One particularly clever trick the British used when they wanted to sell something – the ones in books at least – was to let the customer try it first. When I first arrived in the UK, I was looking forward to seeing one of their least well-known but most highly regarded products. As a teenager I'd read that if you wanted to see for yourself what freedom of expression was, you had to go to Speakers' Corner. I landed at Heathrow on a Saturday night, and first thing on Sunday morning I went straight to Hyde Park. I wasn't especially interested in seeing freedom of expression per se; I knew what it was, at least in theory, although I'd never seen it in action. I was more interested in seeing how those wily Brits went about turning an abstraction into something you could look at and touch, a point on a map that you could go to, a weekly appointment you could attend. Here it was again: that ability to take an idea, turn it into something you could calibrate and measure, and commodify it.

I got lost on my way, because Hyde Park was huge, like a forest in the middle of the city, and its various gates led to neighbourhoods that were miles apart, even though they all looked the same. The passers-by I asked for directions couldn't tell me exactly where freedom of expression was, and some looked baffled by the question. It seemed to me that freedoms were so taken for granted here that people had lost interest and forgotten all about them.

After an hour or more of walking in circles, I found it. It really was a corner, albeit a large one, enclosed by a rank of medium-sized trees that hid it largely from sight. I admired the notion that every freedom should have its own corner; order is a wonderful thing.

From a distance I could make out a small number of speakers; their audience was mostly made up of Asian tourists, who moved briskly from one speaker to the next, taking photos without listening. When I stepped into the corner, I was immediately accosted by a young man carrying a sign that read FREE HUGS, who with great determination was indeed doling out hugs to everybody who walked by.

I felt sorry for the young man, who must have been lonely; I couldn't think of another explanation. But he told me he was spreading happiness. I stepped forward and gave him a warm, heartfelt hug, my first in London, but he didn't seem grateful. He just put his arms mechanically around me for a second or two then moved on to the next customer to repeat the process, a rigid smile on his face. I was saddened, but I tried to think rationally: it wasn't personal, he gave out hundreds of hugs every day, and it must be tiring for him. What an asinine notion of happiness anyway. And you couldn't expect much of something that was handed out for free; there's a reason why expensive things cost more.

A little further on, I stopped to listen to a pensioner standing on a wooden box clutching a Bible. It was taxing to listen to. He was waving his fist in the air and shouting at a frenzied pitch unwarranted by the setting, and spit sprayed from his mouth like a shower of bricks as he warned us of the torment that awaited unbelievers. Nothing he said was new to me, and none of it invited discussion; he spoke with complete conviction, as a believer should. Within two minutes I was bored, and continued a few paces to hear the next speaker, who was also standing on a box. He sounded similar and was spitting a lot too, but the book tucked under his arm was a Qur'an. He also said nothing I didn't know, and left no room for debate, so again I was quickly bored.

Apart from a youth with an American accent who almost convinced me to move to Venezuela to live in a socialist commune but luckily didn't, the speakers all clutched holy books and were saying the same sorts of things about death and the unpleasantness we could expect afterwards. None of them was remarkable except for a short black man holding a Star of David flag at his side. He had quite a crowd of onlookers, and it took me a few minutes to make out what he was talking about. He was excitedly telling the story of Moses and Pharaoh, going through the ten plagues of Egypt one by one; his delivery was compelling and believable, his voice filled with an incomprehensible but nevertheless genuine anger that you couldn't help but empathize with. I stood three rows from the front. Suddenly our eyes met and he looked long and hard at me, then for some reason his features shifted and he began to shout at the top of his voice, calling on his audience to stand with Israel against the Arabs who had enslaved the people of God throughout history. I found myself laughing inwardly, but immediately felt bad, because it wasn't right to mock freedom of expression.

'The Pharaohs weren't Arabs!' shouted someone in the audience derisively. But the short man, undaunted, ignored them, and began to denounce Arabs for enslaving Africans too, whom he said they had kidnapped and sold to the Europeans. Somehow he managed to conclude that Arabs were responsible for all the world's evils – slavery in the Americas, apartheid in South Africa – and he was even audacious enough to claim that the Europeans had learned about slavery from the Muslims. The same man who had spoken interrupted again, this time shouting more loudly: 'The Romans had slaves and they used to feed them to the lions!'

The speaker pretended he hadn't heard. My reaction to this surprised me; I'm shy by nature and avoid speaking in public. I found myself pushing past the people standing in front of me. It wasn't the fact the speaker was talking crap that bothered me, but the way he totally ignored the other person's opinion. In a few seconds I was right at the front, standing directly in front of the man. He stopped speaking and watched closely to see what I was about to do. A heavy silence fell, and I could hear the suspense in the breathing of the people around me. But I didn't know what I was doing or why, or what I should say, and I was about to turn on my heels and flee when my adversary shouted, 'What do you want?'

I didn't know until I was already speaking. 'It's true the Arabs enslaved black people,' I stammered, 'but they enslaved white people too.' Where I had got this bright idea I do not know. But I was pleased with my quick thinking, and added, more confidently: 'They used to kidnap white people and sell them like they did black people.'

Here I was lying through my teeth; I was well aware that the enslavement of the Mamluks was not at all the same as the enslavement of Africans. Africans were enslaved and put to work; Mamluks were destined to rule. But what I learned then about freedom of expression was that saying something, even if it's only half true, is better than silence. I don't know why I thought my comment would set the record straight – other than that there's a certain equality in everyone being treated equally badly, or that some half-lies are more believable than others – but my adversary seemed to have taken my point, even if he didn't comment, only ignored me, took a few steps backward and continued his sermon as if nothing had happened. I noticed a glint of satisfaction in his eyes; schadenfreude, perhaps, directed at those white slaves I'd just mentioned.

I went home that day feeling dispirited at the sorry state freedom of expression was in, and gave up thinking about it for years. I thought I'd never go back to it, until what happened happened and I saw by chance on a huge TV screen in a shopfront on Oxford Street that the masses were out in Tahrir Square. Two days later I found out there were people here protesting outside the Egyptian embassy in solidarity, and decided to join them. I'd never cared about politics in Egypt or anywhere else, to be honest, and the word 'solidarity' gave me the creeps: it sounded arrogant, at best a lazy, watered-down version of doing the right thing. I preferred to do things wholeheartedly or not at all, and so I rarely did anything. But this was an unmissable chance to finally practise freedom of expression, albeit only by showing my 'solidarity', and there is nothing better than doing something for its own sake, without any ulterior motive. As Farid al-Atrash sang: 'Love without hope is the sublimest of all.'

When I went to the embassy for the first time, there were perhaps fifty demonstrators, hemmed in on three sides by metal police barriers. This set-up looked like a corner, which confirmed my sense that there was some kind of relationship in this country between corners and freedom of expression. Not with any basis in law necessarily, but in popular custom and taste. Some people were chanting half-heartedly, while others whispered to one another about what might happen the following day. Two British policewomen stood a short distance away with fixed smiles on their faces.

The embassy door opened without warning and a man emerged holding a cup of tea. He stepped to one side to light a cigarette. A wary silence fell. Then, as he took the first puff, a wave of excitement rippled through the crowd and the chants exploded in volume. The man looked startled. From his clothes and demeanour he was likely only a low-ranking member of staff. Confusion appeared in his eyes, and he glanced curiously at us between sips of his tea. Embarrassing though it is to admit, the sudden appearance of the embassy employee, followed by his swift disappearance back into the building once he'd finished his cigarette – was the most exciting event of the day. The demonstrators were divided: those who'd arrived within the last few years, like me, mostly thought he was a nobody, with no say in anything, but the other half, which included some non-Egyptians as well as Egyptians who'd been born here – these last ones, for some reason, were straight-backed and broad-shouldered, with healthy, rosy cheeks – were filled with rage towards him. He'd dropped his cigarette on the ground and stamped it out with his foot, and this, they said, sullied Egypt's reputation abroad; the two sides got into a heated argument, voices were raised, and it would have turned into a fist fight had not one of the two police officers stepped in to keep the antagonists apart.

Things only quietened down when a young man, one of the straight-backed ones, leaped over one of the metal barriers placed around the protest and strode resolutely towards the embassy. The crowd held their breaths as he approached the front door. He stopped, slowly bent down, and plucked the cigarette butt from the ground before depositing it in the nearest bin. There was a smattering of joyful applause, and the two officers looked pleased.

Sadly, my disappointment that day was no less than on that first Sunday in Hyde Park. By about halfway through the demonstration, I'd realized freedoms are not very exciting. Exercising them isn't fun, at least when there's no risk or threat of punishment involved. I envied people back in Egypt; they had snipers on rooftops, tanks in the streets, camels attacking them in public squares, F16s roaring overhead, cars with diplomatic number plates running them over on pavements. They had a vast range of risks available to be taken, a wide selection of opportunities for heroism. I, though, was too chicken to go back to Cairo.

But it's been said that philosophy is born of disappointment, that discretion is the better part of valour, and that wisdom and envy are siblings. I even came up with a slogan that reflected this experience of mine – quite profoundly, I thought – and one day happened to try it out on one of the protesters standing next to me. He was taken with it, and to my delight began to chant loudly, the other demonstrators soon joining in: 'No repression, no freedom!'

The weekend protests at the embassy went on for months. I personally attended not out of a sense of duty, or for my own satisfaction, but because I was too embarrassed not to. I'd met several of the organizers, and they were terribly nice. I didn't want to disappoint them. They'd also started relying on me to come up with new chants to liven up the protests. This wasn't difficult; I usually took a pair of antonyms – justice and tyranny, say, or dignity and justice – and slotted them into the same structure: two abstract nouns preceded by no, first the one we didn't like, then the one we did. It worked like a charm; the results were always so expressive. I did notice, though, that some people didn't understand what they were shouting and sometimes got the nouns the wrong way around.

Anyway, I kept showing up until what happened happened and the army massacred over twenty Copts at Maspero, and many people felt that what we were doing was pointless, even kind of cheap. Dignity often requires recognizing that one is impotent and ineffectual; there was no point being stubborn. Plus, the embassy receptionist had stopped coming outside to smoke during our protests, and that took all the fun away. My chants had come to sound predictable, and enthusiasm for them diminished. Weeks went by. Nobody noticed my absence; I forgot about the embassy people and they forgot about me. I stopped following the news from Egypt because it depressed me. Over time, the demonstrations in London and then in Cairo fizzled out altogether. I started spending my weekends at the gym instead.

The gym made up for my second run-in with freedom of expression. There was a large sign at the entrance which said NO PAIN NO GAIN; it felt familiar. I went up to one of the staff, a tall, muscular young man in neon sportswear with the words PERSONAL TRAINER emblazoned across his chest, and asked him who'd come up with the slogan. He said he had no idea; probably some philosopher. It was well known and had been around since forever, and sometimes when a saying becomes too popular, the person who came up with it gets forgotten. I liked the idea that a person could be a victim of their own success; that their own wisdom could become their rival. The muscly young man advised me to do everything in moderation, including pain and gain. And success, I added. His words seemed pretty deep – after all, personal trainers are the sages of our times – so I told him about my political slogans and how I came up with them. He nodded appreciatively and agreed they bore a resemblance to the slogan of the unknown philosopher, then remarked that politics was essentially the same as working out, and that the gym was like life. Or maybe the other way round, I don't remember.

With time I came to see that the gym was indeed like politics, but upside down. When I was running on the treadmill, looking down at the moving band beneath my feet, I imagined it to be the caterpillar tread of a tank turned on its back and myself to be running away from it, or stamping on it with all my might. Without a doubt, what gave me the impetus to work out every day was the fact it righted the wrongs of the outside world, turning its logic on its head. It was enough for me that I could run for hours without ever getting anywhere.

But the real turning point was when I truly understood the sign in the gym toilets. On the inside of each cubicle door was the charming phrase EVERY SQUAT COUNTS. It was a motivational quote, on the face of it, that encouraged you to keep working out even when you weren't at the gym, and it always made me smile as I dropped my trousers to sit down on the toilet. But on one such occasion a few years ago, when I was getting terrible constipation from the protein supplements I was taking, and straining as hard as I could to get the job done, the true meaning revealed itself to me at my time of greatest pain.

Every squat counted. Every step a person took, every little movement made around the office or the house, every breath that entered the lungs, every exhalation, every time you had sex, every calorie you consumed or burned, every step of a staircase, everything: everything had to be carefully, dutifully counted. You take the gym with you when you go out into the world, and slowly the world itself becomes one big gym. I left the toilet that day, entered the weights room and looked around me to see others like me, their faces marked with the same sense of helplessness. We were a part of the same brotherhood, though we didn't exchange a word. Our aim was to purify and discipline the body. When everything was senseless and out of control, when armoured vehicles were crushing people in the streets and we couldn't do anything about it, all we had power over was our own bodies. We could defy them, subjugate them, bend them to our will; we could use them to conquer iron, to vanquish hunger and greed; we could parade them before the mirrors that lined the walls. There's no point looking for the meaning of life, because there's probably no such thing. Just look for some way to make it worthwhile. That's what I was doing.

So when I spoke to Kayode, it cheered me up, even though he sounded tired and broken, like he was getting in touch to tell me the world was ending. After finishing with the Cotton Man and leaving the hospital, I'd walked aimlessly around Whitechapel for a while. I wandered through the market near the Underground station, feeling at home among the brown faces and the clamour of the vegetable stalls, the headscarved women bustling around them, the smell of curry, the boxes of fish sitting in ice with flies hovering over them; these things were strange to me, and yet so familiar at the same time, like they'd come from a half-remembered dream whose forgotten half kept me awake at nights. My eyes met those of an older man with an orange beard, Bangladeshi I assumed, and I smiled and nodded a greeting. He smiled warily back. 'Salam aleikum, brother,' he said soberly. It sent a shiver of joy through me that dissipated within a few paces.

My feet led me next to Whitechapel Mosque, and there I took out my phone to find a long string of unread messages from Kayode, all asking the same thing. I had to deal with it, so I called him back. As I expected, he was full of bad news and wanted to meet up immediately. I told him I couldn't meet him anywhere near the office because I'd called in sick, but I was happy to meet him somewhere else after working hours. Kayode suggested we meet at six in Greenwich, in front of the Royal Observatory.

Greenwich. That was what cheered me up. It was only twenty minutes from the house by bike; it wasn't a long or tiring trip, but it still burned a hundred and fifty calories each way. Three hundred calories: two tins of tuna, or forty grammes of protein, an adult male's recommended daily allowance. This calculation flickered automatically through my head, reassuring me that every squat counted and that there were simple reasons to be happy. I'd done this calculation hundreds of times, because nobody knew where Brockley was or had even heard of it. And I was proud to say I lived twenty minutes from Greenwich, the revered meridian that divided the world into East and West; twenty minutes from point zero, twenty minutes from the hour the planet set its clocks by, twenty minutes from the centre of everything. Greenwich was my favourite place to meet people or go for a stroll, and whenever I made the trip, I'd quickly add up the calories and feel happy.

The hot July sun was still high in the sky when I set out on my bike, but my attempts at distracting myself from what Kayode had told me only worked for a few minutes, and I was quickly engulfed by dark thoughts again. The night before, mere hours after we'd visited her, he'd told me during our short phone call, Service User A had been found dead, her body badly burned. What's more, the fire appeared to have started in her room and had consumed the entire basement; some people were still in hospital. The police were involved, and the hostel had been closed and the residents moved to temporary accommodation. A major investigation was under way, and the media would no doubt soon get hold of the story. Who knows where it would go then. Kayode was certain she had killed herself after our visit, and if the connection were to be made and our names brought up in the inquiry, that would be the end of us. Just two low-level council employees: we would be the perfect scapegoats. Everybody else could go to bed with a clear conscience, and things would go back to normal.

I didn't know what was going through Kayode's head, but there probably wasn't a lot we could do at this point. The busy ride to Greenwich didn't give me much chance to think; it was half past five, right in the middle of rush hour. I got there a few minutes early to give myself time to lock up my bike. I always looked for a spot in full view, and used two locks. Bicycle thefts were so common in London now – a new bike would barely last two or three months before it disappeared. No cyclist had felt safe since the government embarked on its austerity policies.

Locking the bike up a way from the Observatory, I walked along the river for a while, feeling slightly annoyed at how busy it was. The whole area, especially the parks, was packed with families spending the sunny day outside. When I headed for the Observatory, I spotted Kayode waiting for me. He was smiling as usual. I gave him a wave, but the sun was in his eyes and it took him a few seconds to notice me coming towards him. He opened his arms in greeting and drew me into a warm embrace, patting my shoulder vigorously as he always did.

'How are you, my favourite friend?'

Before I could respond, he grasped my hand forcefully, as if to wring it dry, and began towing me towards the front of the Observatory. Without saying anything, he took a few steps to the right, then smartly back to the left, still pulling me carefully behind him. He stopped for a few seconds as if trying to remember something, then looked searchingly down at the ground. Suddenly, his features broke into the expression of one who has found the object of a long and arduous search, his eyes glinting in delight, and he stood erect on the spot, his feet planted wide apart. It wasn't hard to work out what he was doing, but it seemed frivolous given the circumstances, and childish for a man of Kayode's age.

'You know why I asked you to meet me here?' Kayode asked. 'Because here we can put one foot in the east of the world and one in the west. Look, this foot is on the east of the Greenwich meridian, and this one's on the west.

London's always been very self-important, and its rulers thought they were the centre of the world, so they decided to divide the entire earth and sky into two right here. Such arrogance! But that means nothing to us, as you know. People like you and me will always be in-between in this city. Neither here nor there.'

I sensed one of Kayode's grand theories in the offing, but I wasn't really listening. It was much too hot for pointless philosophizing.

'Have you brought me here to look at the meridian?'

A frown flickered momentarily across Kayode's face, before his indulgent smile reappeared.

'No, no. I just know it's near where you live, and I like it here, so I thought it would be a good place to meet. Believe it or not, this was the first place I visited when I arrived in London thirty years ago. I studied geography at university in Lagos, you know. And the only thing I wanted to see in London was time itself – the thin line where it disappears, where the minutes swallow themselves. I came here, still a young man, and looked at the golden strip on the ground inside the Observatory that marks the prime meridian, and I saw time lying there on both sides in submission. I felt so proud and so sad, all at once.'

There was a note of genuine emotion in Kayode's voice. I didn't understand why, but it embarrassed me, and I thought it would only be polite to share some of my own memories so we'd be on an equal footing.

'I know what you mean,' I said. 'When I first got here, the thing I wanted to see most was Speakers' Corner, and it was a total disappointment.'

I thought he hadn't heard me, because he was staring into the distance, and there was a brief silence before he turned to look at me. 'Speakers' Corner!' he exclaimed sadly. 'I've never been there. Let's go and find somewhere to sit on the grass.'

We strolled for a little while in the park until Kayode pointed out a spot near a large tree spreading its shade over a wide patch of ground. He suggested with a chuckle that we sit on the border between light and shade, to maintain our in-between status. I didn't object. He placed his bag on the grass and sat on it so as not to stain his trousers, then turned to me, his features set in a grave expression I'd never seen on his smiling face before.

'Let's get down to business. The woman took her own life, and if we're interviewed for any kind of inquiry, they'll figure out she expressed suicidal thoughts during her meeting with us, which means we should have immediately raised a safeguarding concern. It's also possible they'll claim that some of the things we told her about the assessment and the results might have contributed to her death. Either way, they'll blame the whole thing on us. At the very least, we'll lose our jobs, and nobody will ever employ us again.'

Kayode's calm, composed manner sent a small shiver down my spine. I felt cold prickles of sweat breaking out on my forehead.

'And in the worst-case scenario, we might be charged with wilful neglect, which carries a maximum prison sentence of—'

'So what do we do?' I interrupted.

Kayode registered the note of panic in my voice with a certain satisfaction. 'Don't worry, it's not as complicated as it might seem,' he said in the same controlled voice. 'All we have to do is remove her name from our records. We can delete everything from the system. We'll pretend Service User A never existed. And then no inquiry will come anywhere near us.'

For a second I thought he was joking, but his face and voice were utterly serious. He'd lost the plot.

'What are you talking about?' I said. 'Her name appears in hundreds of databases. There are dozens of agencies involved – psychiatric hospitals, prisons, the Home Office, social services, housing, the DWP, her GP. She has a son, and a family. And there's a burned dead body. What are you going to do about all that?'

Kayode returned to his habitual smile and placed a reassuring hand on my shoulder. The gesture irritated me and I pushed his hand politely but firmly away. 'Listen,' he said confidently. 'People like that have no life beyond these databases. They don't exist outside of the system. Anyway, you misunderstand me. Obviously I don't mean we should pretend she never existed at all. That wouldn't be possible. But we don't need to. I just want to delete any trace of her contact with us, remove the records of our visit.'

I considered it for a second, but I was quickly overwhelmed by a renewed panic. If we were found out, the consequences would be unimaginable. It was fraud. Still, I found myself entertaining his proposal.

'How are you going to do that? What if people find out?'

Kayode smiled even more broadly and leaned back on the grass. He seemed to have come prepared for everything I might ask.

'It's easy, my friend. The records are our records. We're the ones who write them and keep them. We sign off on them. And they speak in our voice, not hers. People like her don't get a voice. Even when we write down what they say, we put it in our words and our handwriting. We choose the vocabulary and the tone to suit our purposes. Those records are there to protect us, no more and no less. We might be on the bottom rung of the ladder, but in this respect we have a certain power, and it's our prerogative to use it, just this once, to protect ourselves.'

I was disgusted by what he was saying, all the more so because it was true. But the fact it was true didn't mean we should take advantage of it.

'What you're saying is wrong, Kayode,' I said. 'You know that.'

For the first time since we'd met that day, his face looked angry, or perhaps afraid. 'Listen, my friend,' he said, pleading now. 'I have three children. My youngest is in junior school. I'm still paying off a mortgage. I can't go back to Nigeria. It's too late. We've never done anything for ourselves, we've never achieved anything, you or me. The only thing keeping us here, and plenty of other people too, is the shame that would await us if we went home with nothing. All I have left is the hope that I can retire there, and sit in the sun when I'm old. A house with a swimming pool is going to be the pay-off for all the years I've wasted here, and all the years I still have left to waste. Now, that poor woman lived a truly wretched life, and that's neither your fault nor mine. Nobody even cares. Her own son put her in prison. Our managers don't pay any attention to people like her, except when they turn into dead bodies, and then they have to find someone to blame. I don't want to be that person. And neither do you.'

He was absolutely correct. I told myself again that just because something was correct, that didn't make it right; truth was not necessarily fair. And yet I could feel myself becoming more and more entangled in his scheme.

'I could remove our visit from the system, like you say. But that wouldn't be enough. We'd easily be caught out. They'd find out sooner or later.'

I could see Kayode was gathering his strength ready to make a final stand. He wanted to settle the matter there and then.

'The truth is what we want it to be. The truth is what everybody agrees on for the sake of the greater good. You saw – there's no actual line either inside the Royal Observatory or outside of it. But everyone believes in it. Every single place on the planet and in the sky is measured in relation to it. The entire world sets its clocks by it. The meridian isn't a real thing, and yet it still exists, because people agree it does.'

I'd had enough of Kayode's idiotic philosophizing, and his self-satisfied tone of voice infuriated me.

'Kayode!' I almost shouted. 'It's not sheer coincidence that the meridian runs past the Royal Naval College. This is where all the country's admirals were educated. This is the place from which Great Britain ruled the high seas. The meridian doesn't run through here because people agree it does, like you're saying. It runs through here because these people had bigger cannons than everyone else.'

His features went slack in apparent resignation. There was a frightening silence. I wanted his plan to work, I really did; I just wanted it to be a better plan. I exhaled in relief when he started to speak again.

'You're right. Let's forget about the meridian for now. Let me tell you a few things you don't know about, because you weren't around. Please bear with me. When I came to this country, I thought I was going to be a geographer. Of course, that didn't happen. The only job I could find, after months of searching, was as a nurse in London's last lunatic asylum. It was in Bromley, south of here. Those places were huge institutions, home to hundreds, maybe thousands of people. People were born there, they got married there, they died there. The one where I worked was a fully fledged ghetto, with its own version of apartheid. A mix of the mentally ill, alcoholics, petty criminals, decrepit homeless people, the lot. At first I didn't understand why the nurses were all immigrants with dark skin. But over time I saw that when there was trouble, we were the ones who had to deal with it. We had to do the things nobody else wanted to do. There was a lot of violence, a lot of screaming. Bones got broken. When Thatcher brought in "care in the community", and closed all the asylums and let everybody out, we were sent out after them. The battle was moved away from the ghetto, into the streets and people's homes, and the violence became less visible. But it's still there. That's why you and I are here now – because it's chaos down here, and nobody up there wants to get their hands dirty. We've been left to deal with things however we see fit. Nobody above us cares what happens down here. It doesn't matter to them if one more woman kills herself. Battles always involve a few casualties. As long as everything's hushed up, as long as there's no outcry, nobody will care. Trust me, everybody will be glad to forget about the whole thing. You and I can win this one.'

We didn't talk any more that evening. I said goodbye to him and promised to think about it and let him know in the morning. He headed off towards the Underground, and I walked back along the Thames to the spot where I'd locked my bike. When I got there, any faith I might have had in our ability to win battles disintegrated entirely. The lock had been broken open and was lying on the ground, and where my bike had been was an empty space.

7

Adam was four years older than me, and now I was exactly the age he'd been. The astonishing thing was that the next day, I'd be older than him – by one day. Time had stopped for him that night, at the age of forty, and it never moved again. Xiang Hu was in the shower when Adam called me for the last time, on Messenger. He asked if I was free for a chat, said he needed to get some things off his chest. We never used to be friends at all when I lived in Cairo; we had a tense relationship which involved some flattery but was mainly a site of bullying and competitiveness. Back then, every encounter between two people was an opportunity to take revenge on the outside world. When he got married a few months before I left, he didn't invite me to the wedding, and I didn't speak to him for years.

I don't know what happened then. It took us a while, but we became Facebook friends after some conciliatory gestures on his part. You never know what time will do to people, or where Facebook will take them. I observed him from a distance as the days went by, watched his kids growing up in the pictures he posted. He seemed more delicate with the wrinkles age had brought. I could see his marriage falling apart in the face of his wife, who smiled less and less as time went by. Meanwhile, he counted the white hairs that appeared more and more thickly in each of my photos and told me, when I went back to Cairo for visits, that I looked like an old man. He told me to wear bright, busy clothes like he did: that was the secret to staying young and living long. In the messages we exchanged, I discovered that all his former hostility had been bravado. He had been a lonely, frightened child acting out, building a shelter in which to hide from his own fragility. Now finally we were far enough apart to be Facebook friends. There in the realm of blue faces, where everything could be so easily concealed from those around us, we buried our misgivings and replaced them with affection. We laid ourselves bare without fear. And when he got divorced, we started speaking every day, sometimes more than once. I'd see his big, powerful body on my screen, shaking as he sobbed like a little child. When he asked me that day if we could Skype, I knew he wanted to cry. He wanted me to witness his defeat and share his grief over the life that had slipped from his grasp. But I was busy.

'From Taiwan?' he echoed. 'How did you meet her?!'

I couldn't remember how I'd met Olivia. On the apps, or through mutual friends. Something like that. I'd quoted my aunt's infamous saying about Formosa and she'd laughed so hard she practically passed out. 'Your aunt sounds mad,' she said, and gave me her number.

She had two names, Olivia and Xiang Hu. The first was the white name printed in her passport: palatable to

Westerners, easy to pronounce and remember. That was the name she carried with her when she travelled, the one she hid behind like she was one of them. The second was her real name, which she didn't usually share with anyone in London.

'Surely you have a Chinese name?' I'd asked her.

I called her by her Chinese name, and she liked that. She came home with me after our second date.

'Hey, is it true they're tight like people say?'

He said it with childlike innocence, then sniggered, caught by surprise at his own vulgarity. All the dejection of a minute ago had dissipated. I had to disappoint him: no, it wasn't true, as with most of the things people said about women.

'OK, but are the guys there small? Haven't you asked her?'

I actually had asked her at some point, but she said she didn't know. She'd never slept with an Asian guy; she liked them but they didn't turn her on. She'd only slept with white guys, when she was in Australia. Only white men turned her on, and for some reason I turned her on like a white man. I found this a bit insulting. She didn't understand why I wasn't grateful; she was sure I'd be pleased. But I wasn't too upset; it had worked out in my favour after all.

'OK, man, I'll leave you with the girl. But we have to speak tomorrow morning, OK?'

Xiang Hu and I wore ourselves out that night, and it was well into the afternoon by the time we woke up. I opened my eyes, picked up my phone and checked Facebook, like I always do first thing.

Adam Mahmoud al-Sharqawi died early this morning of a heart attack. The funeral will be held at al-Rahma mosque in Ayn Shams this evening at 7.

That was his full name, I was absolutely sure, but I couldn't believe it. I thought I must have misread. I doubted myself for a moment, and tried to say his name in full in my head, but I couldn't. I felt the cold hand of helplessness closing around my neck. I was lying on the floor next to Xiang Hu, and I started to sob. Everything was mixed up inside my head. I looked at her and didn't know who she was. I looked again and again, through a cloud of tears, at the two sentences our mutual friend had written on his page. I could still make out each word in isolation, but my mind had stopped working, and I couldn't take in the sum total of what they meant. I lost control of my body; my arms and legs trembled violently. I gulped loudly, desperately trying to catch my breath as I fought the weight pressing down on my chest. Xiang Hu was aghast at the sight of me lying shaking and sobbing on the floor. She scrambled to the front door half-dressed, clutching the other half of her clothes, and I never saw her again.

I messaged our mutual friend to ask. He replied straight away. Yes, it was 'our Adam'. But that couldn't induce me to believe it. I went to Adam's own page. There were hundreds of tributes and condolences posted on his wall. They were meaningless. There was not a single thing on earth or in heaven which could have convinced me then that Adam was dead.

Then I opened up our Messenger conversations. His last message was right there at the top, and his profile photo – smiling and bursting with life – was unchanged. Nothing was different. I stared at his face for a while, then began rereading our messages. He was right here; he hadn't gone anywhere. I waited to see if he'd type something. Again, tears welled up from deep in my chest and took hold, so hard I could hear them knocking on my ribcage. 'I wish I'd called you!' I gasped. 'If only I'd called you!'

It was the first time I'd seen the enormity of death up close: when all doors close in the face of your regrets, the path behind you crumbles away, and whatever time there was left for fixing things runs out. There's no use wishing you could go back to things that will never be. This *never*, I realized, was the watchword of death, and its infinity referred to the powerlessness of the living. Regret over things we never shared with those we've lost. Grief at things still to come that we'll never be able to tell them about, or share a laugh over. Many obscure things became clear to me then, like why the ancients believed eternity came only in death and immortality could be achieved only in oblivion.

Apparently some people only need a few hours, maybe days, to get past the stage of denial. For me it took weeks. I would open our message conversations, write to him and wait for him to reply. I'd stare at the screen for hours and read every word we'd written to each other in the last ten years.

Ayman called me daily. 'You're all by yourself over there,' he'd say. 'Here we've got each other for support. Grief is meant to be shared.'

He'd also say, 'Adam is dead, man. He's not going to message you. You have to accept it.'

Ayman was the last thing I had left of Cairo now Adam was gone. He told me I should take a break from Facebook. I did try, but I could never go more than a few hours. Writing to Adam was my only relief. At first, I expected him to reply, but over time, our one-sided conversation came to be enough. I possessed a warm, reassuring conviction – where it came from, I have no idea – that he was reading what I wrote, and it made him happy. As the weeks went by, it became clear to me that Facebook was a breath of divine mercy sent down to humankind. It was the gentle touch of a compassionate hand on our hearts. It brought loved ones together across vast distances and made their separation bearable; it remained loyal, forever, to the memory of the ones we had lost.

People didn't die on Facebook. Their pages remained unchanged and their photos didn't age. Their conversations and their quarrels, every embarrassing thing they'd posted in moments of despair, remained fresh and green like it had just been written, seemed to get fresher and more vivid with the passing of time. I thought this was unintentional at first, but soon realized it wasn't at all. Facebook would remind me insistently of his birthday every year, and of our friendship anniversary, adding a year each time to the years we'd known and loved each other, which would last for ever. It doggedly, loyally reminded me of photos we'd been tagged in together, posts I'd written to him or about him, links he'd shared with me. The act of remembering filled me with gratitude and faith.

My acquaintances mostly thought I'd lost the plot when I told them there was something divine about Facebook, and that we were immortal now thanks to its gifts. The messages we wrote on its walls and the memories associated with our icons would be our lasting legacies. They'd be lessons to those who came after us and never knew us. They'd be our connection with the tomorrow that we'd never see but that would see us. It wasn't Facebook alone that I venerated and began to treat with the proper reverence; I came to see the hidden meaning in databases and networks and archives and all the other systems of digital immortality on which we left our imprint each day, often without realizing it, and almost always with an insouciance born of short-sightedness.

As I made my way home from Greenwich after saying goodbye to Kayode, the memory of Adam tormented me. Who was I to tamper with the system and sully the memory of the dead? Of course I wouldn't dare delete Service User A's entry from the database. I didn't care what might happen, or what the consequences would be for Kayode or me. There was no sin more wicked than deliberate forgetting.

The realization that I couldn't go through with Kayode's plan filled me with a rush of reassurance, and my feelings of anger at the loss of my bike gave way to a placid contentment and acceptance of whatever the world might have in store. I had no choice but to travel by public transport now. The station wasn't far, and the streets were less busy than they had been, which added to my sense of serenity. I was amazed by the speed with which my mood had transformed.

A light evening breeze tempered the residual heat of the day as I walked down the main road. I took a long, deep breath, and a wave of warm, humid air hit me in the face, heavy with a scent that made me long for late summer evenings in Cairo. The sight of people strolling peaceably along the pavements and shouting tipsily at each other as they gathered outside pubs and bars, their lean, sunburned bodies in bright summer clothes, was joyous and beautiful. Everything was so brilliant it hurt. I thought it was the most exquisite scene I had ever beheld. I gazed at the handsome faces and bodies, which aroused in me both envy and lust. At the Tube station, the atmosphere was carnivalesque. The pavements heaved with gorgeous women and just as gorgeous men of every colour and race and language, and everyone was holding hands and exchanging kisses hot with the ebullience of alcohol. In one corner, a teenage couple stood touching each other with delicate, tender fingertips, their eyes filled with a timid, quivering desire.

I hadn't taken public transport since the first round of austerity, when they'd cut my salary, and I got lost trying to find my platform. The layout of the station had changed. The recorded announcements they played over the loud-speakers every few minutes came less often now: 'If you see something that doesn't look right, speak to staff or text British Transport Police.' There hadn't been any terrorist attacks in the city for a while; maybe they'd stopped for good, or maybe they were just getting less frequent. Maybe people were simply resigned to them. These disheartening announcements didn't really seem necessary.

It was a few minutes before my train arrived. There weren't many people on it, but I stood instead of sitting down. The idea of sitting up close to other people on public transport had come to seem a bit awkward. The train remained at the platform for a few minutes, and another announcement played, articulating the city's newest fear: 'There are beggars and buskers operating on this train. Please do not encourage their presence by supporting them.'

The announcement played twice before the train moved away. The wording wasn't kind, and I felt a shiver of unease. At the next stop, the announcement played again, more loudly, this time accompanied by a long shriek of feedback. There was obviously something up with the PA system; passengers were putting their hands over their ears, and some of them closed their eyes and screwed up their faces in discomfort. I thought to myself that begging was preferable to terrorism, and to bike theft, especially in an era of austerity.

I went back to gazing hungrily at the handsome faces around me in the train carriage. Opposite me was a beautiful young Asian woman, with a face like an angel and long, glossy hair. Our gazes met. Her eyes were wide and filled with both surprise and an alluring confidence. She smiled straight at me, which didn't happen to me often, and I smiled back. Suddenly, her features contorted into a hard frown and she gave me a look of fear mixed with anger, before turning to face the other direction. Then she burst out laughing, then began to dance, and I realized she was tripping.

My phone buzzed in my trouser pocket, and I was taking it out to look at the message notification when a searing putrid smell hit me from behind and I felt a hand fall heavily on my shoulder.

'Spare any change? I'm hungry and I've got nowhere to sleep tonight.'

When I turned around, the man's face was extremely close to my own, and the foul smell he gave off was so intense I took a step backwards without even meaning to. It was a pungent mixture of sweat, alcohol and cigarettes, and for a second I couldn't catch my breath. I automatically lifted a hand to cover my nose and mouth.

'Sorry mate, I haven't got any cash on me,' I replied. It was true; I didn't have a single penny. Who used cash these days? But he was insistent. He put his other hand on my other shoulder and asked again, in a trustworthy Scottish accent, like people say here. I believed him, and I could see he needed help, but I didn't have any cash on me. I apologized again, making more obvious expressions of concern and regret, and wished him a good evening. He staggered drunkenly away from me and turned his attention to the other passengers.

'Spare any change? I'm homeless and hungry, and I need help.'

The sight was truly dreadful. He was wearing three layers of thick clothes despite the heat, perhaps everything he owned, all stained with mud and sweat patches. His swollen feet, bare and with long, grubby toenails, poked out of his sandals like they were about to explode. His red beard was covered in trails of saliva and mucus, and the skin on his hands and neck was thick with old, festering scabs. I felt a shiver of pity and revulsion, but there was nothing I could do for him, so I turned away and looked at my phone.

Hi, the body will arrive at Nunhead Cemetery, Islamic section, around 12.30 p.m. tomorrow. No ceremony but you can attend the burial if you want. Patrick.

For a few seconds I couldn't think who Patrick was, until I collected my thoughts and realized it must be the Cotton Man. Who else could it be? I couldn't remember if he'd ever told me his name. It didn't matter anyway. The message evoked mixed feelings. Should I be pleased to have received the news? Or sad? This was a problem I'd been having a lot over the last few years. I often couldn't identify the appropriate emotion for a given situation, or even the inappropriate emotion; I simply couldn't distinguish between the two. At other times, my emotions would turn 180 degrees in the space of a few moments. I thought the best thing to do was probably to text Ayman straight away to let him know.

'My name's James. I'm hungry and alone, and I need your help.'

The homeless man had returned after walking the length of the carriage. None of the passengers looked at him. Everyone was making themselves busy with their phones or staring into the distance. The girl on drugs had stopped dancing, closed her eyes and was pretending to sleep standing up. There are some things people are good at not seeing, things it's better for them not to know. I hazarded a guess that James wasn't his real name; he'd chosen an ordinary, classic name with nothing special about it, one that would convey that he was just like everybody else, that he could be someone we knew, and that what had happened to him could happen to anybody. Names give people faces, even if we avoid looking at them. The man approached me again, and repeated his request. I was annoyed at his insistence, and by the smell; he wasn't seeking our compassion, no, he wanted to spoil our journey and sully our unspoken compact of beauty. It was extortion! We had to pay him to disappear from sight. Bribe him to stop ruining our evening and making everyone in our little microcosm feel uncomfortable. I turned my face and went back to staring at my phone screen, doing nothing in particular. Suddenly, a heavy, dull shove knocked me sideways, my mobile flew through the air, and I found myself spreadeagled on the floor of the carriage.

'I'm talking to you, Paki scum!' yelled the man. 'Put your fucking phone away!'

He'd pushed me over with all his strength and was shouting in a frenzy. I was terrified he was going to jump on me and beat me up. I wouldn't stand a chance; he was big and his fist, clenched in acrimonious readiness, looked powerful enough to shatter the bones in my face with a single punch. A kick in the stomach with that huge foot might kill me.

The brakes squealed and we pulled into the next station, where the man leaped out as soon as the doors opened, dashed down the platform and disappeared from sight.

'Are you OK? Do you need some help?'

It was the woman on drugs, who'd been roused by the sound of my head hitting the floor. Her face bore such an exaggerated expression of terror I almost laughed. I told her I was OK. She bent down to pick up my phone, handed it back to me and offered me her other arm to help me to my feet. I didn't need it, and stood up easily, but I could feel my knees trembling slightly and there was a faint ringing in my ears. The nearest passenger moved his bag from the seat beside him so I could sit down. A tense silence descended on the carriage. The other passengers avoided looking at me and each other, and I did the same. I was thankful the situation hadn't escalated further, but inside I felt shaken.

I picked up a newspaper from the next seat and buried my face in it along with my feelings of humiliation. I skimmed the headlines on the front page; none of the articles looked like they were worth reading. A light item in the bottom corner caught my eye – TEN PER CENT OF PETS IN UK HAVE THEIR OWN BEDROOM – and I read it to distract myself, smiling.

I called Ayman as soon as I got home, and recounted the unpleasant evening I'd had, from the meeting with Kayode to the unprovoked attack. 'Serves you right,' he sniggered.

'But why?' I exclaimed. 'What did I do to deserve it?'

'What are you so upset about, the fact he called you Pakistani? Or the fact he called you scum?'

'Come on, man. Both of them. And he didn't call me Pakistani, he called me "Paki". It's a slur.'

'What did you expect?' he replied. 'What, you're surprised people call you names? Go abroad and they'll give you a hard time. I told you that ages ago.'

'OK, and I could have listened to you and stayed in shitty Egypt. You think I wouldn't be having a hard time there too?'

'Sure,' he said, in a different tone. He wasn't sneering or joking now. Or rather, he wasn't hiding what he meant behind a veneer of sarcasm. 'Like they say, a deadbeat at home is a deadbeat abroad. So stop complaining.'

His words landed harder than the fists of the man on the Tube.

'For Christ's sake, I'm not complaining!' I was raising my voice now. 'I'm just telling you. Anyway, if I can't complain to you, how am I supposed to get it off my chest? You know I don't have anyone here to tell. Why are you being so harsh about it? What are you annoyed about?'

The anger in my voice seemed to set us back on course. 'Hey, no need to get mad,' he said. 'How are things with you anyway? What are you going to do about the woman? The one that killed herself?'

I didn't understand the question. I'd already told Ayman I wasn't going to entertain Kayode's idea. And I was pretty sure he'd share my view, because he'd always been one to do things by the book.

'What do you mean, what am I going to do? There's nothing to be done. Que sera sera.'

He went silent for a few moments. I wasn't sure why. But when he spoke, his voice held all the weariness he'd been concealing behind his taunting a minute earlier.

'Listen, the woman's dead. And that's not your fault, either of you. You need to put the living first. If it really is easy like he says, and there's no risk involved, then do it – delete anything that's going to have people asking questions. Close the door that's letting in the cold and give yourself a break. You know the saying.'

'What's up with you today? You sound like Auntie in the village with all these proverbs!'

Ayman laughed, this time at himself. We'd swapped roles; it was my turn to have a dig at him now. That was usually how we smoothed things over.

'Yeah, well, they also say that he who forgets his roots is lost. Listen to me for once. Stop being so stubborn. Why pick this hill to die on? Don't make the same mistake as me. I'm always acting the hero. I stayed here to look after Dad because he's old, he's got no one else, whatever. And look at me now. I haven't slept since that stuff with Ghiyath's parents. I'm tired, man. I feel so fucking useless. What am I even doing here? Nothing. I've never got anything done.'

It wasn't the first time Ayman had expressed doubts over his decision to stay in Egypt. He'd won the green card lottery at one point, years ago, but decided not to leave, and he'd been tormented by pangs of regret ever since. But his voice now had a heavy bitterness I didn't recognize, a note of despair that didn't fit the image of him I'd hung on to all these years. I got the impression his insistence that I should go along with Kayode's plan was in fact his own declaration of surrender. I didn't know what to say.

'You're doing fine,' Ayman sighed. 'You've got a house and a job. You go to sleep at night feeling safe in your own bed. Just get on with it. Don't lose your job. You don't know what it's like here these days. Thank the Lord, you're better off than most people.'

Ayman's words had an envious ring. I muttered something in feigned agreement; it was pointless complaining to him about my life here. It was no use telling him there was only one thing keeping me in London: the fact I had nowhere else to go. I could hardly go back to where I came from. If Cairo had stayed how it was ten years ago, then I might have. But I was stuck here like he was stuck there. Enough had changed to make me a stranger in Cairo, a stranger to Cairo, but not enough had changed in me to wash away the mark of a stranger I bore in London. Everything here was temporary and in-between, just like everything there was suffocating and grim. And waiting was often worse than despair, though he didn't know that. Life was a long battle against forgetting, a constant effort to hold on to the past, to summon it up in the wrong time and the wrong place. I knew he wouldn't understand that trying to escape and failing, then trying again, was easier to bear than being nostalgic for captivity. He wouldn't be able to grasp that longing to be rescued was better than being rescued and realizing it was a trick. I understood why he wouldn't understand, and I forgave him.

We ended the call, his words leaving me feeling dazed and uncertain. I didn't know what I should do the next day about Service User A and her data. I was worried about what would happen if I got fired. I felt an overwhelming urge to cry. But the tears sat stubbornly in my eyes and refused to flow, defying me and my sadness.

I left my bedroom, went through to the kitchen and got down on my knees to open the freezer. I opened the top drawer and stared into it for a few seconds, but that's all it took. One look was enough for the tears to surge, warm and reassuring, from my eyes. It was the bag of frozen onion rings that did it. I reached out a hand and brushed away the thin layer of frost covering the plastic, and the hardness holding back the grief melted away. It always amazed me how sorrows kept each other company like they were tied together by a fine thread, how the memories followed each other in such quick succession.

Potitsa had left six months ago. She had left me a lot to remember her by: four years of intimate things, marks of familiarity we'd accumulated day by day, hand in hand, before our eyes and in our souls. The rocking chair in the living room was a birthday present from her two years ago. The wardrobe, she'd bought when she moved in. Over there was the corner where she liked to sit and read in the evenings. We'd brought the carpet back from India together; I didn't like it at all, but I was proud I'd haggled and got it for half the original price. I could still hear peals of laughter erupting from behind the door; there was nobody who could laugh with the embarrassed innocence of Potitsa sitting on the toilet. This was her side of the bed, which she kept warm on lazy winter mornings. There were five cups left out of the half-dozen set I'd brought from Cairo; she'd broken one in our first month together, and I'd been so angry about it we nearly broke up. Whenever I opened the front door, I'd remember how she used to wait for me on nights I came in late; I'd turn the key in the lock to find her standing there, sleepy and a little worried, and she'd put her arms around me.

It was me who said we should break up. I don't even remember why. I said we should separate; she cried a little, then left. That's how quietly relationships here came to an end. She slipped away without any fuss or a single word of blame, and she left behind our entire life together. I wished she'd scream or throw something at me, swear at me, but she didn't. How could it all be so simple? Sometimes I cried to make myself feel less guilty, and sometimes I cried in regret. I'd look at it all and see nothing but the end of the world, or the ruins of the tribe's encampment, as they put it in classical poetry. There was nothing worse than having the ruins inside your own flat. In the freezer. Every break-up was like a little death. And every death was the end of a world, a unique world whose features would never recur in that combination again. It was gone for good. It couldn't be recovered or replaced or resurrected. Other relationships would come along, sure, or maybe not, but what was certain was that the past was over and done with. When I looked back at all those little bereavements, my only consolation was my own singularity, a dark and nebulous notion we could only understand through loss. It turned a bag of frozen onion into an emblem of love lost and a witness to the separation.

She'd bought the onion rings two weeks before we broke up, like she knew. She could feel it in her heart. She'd used at least half of them, I don't know when, and left the other half. The morning she left, she'd told me it was easy: you just put them in the oven on 180 degrees for half an hour. She looked at me fondly, told me to eat properly and not start smoking again, squeezed my shoulder, then left. Six

147

months had gone by since then, and the onion rings were still sitting in the top drawer of the freezer like a corpse, its ghosts hovering around it. I didn't like deep-fried onion rings and I absolutely hated how they smelled. More than once, I thought about chucking them away, but my hands wouldn't do it. If I didn't have the onion rings, what would I do when I needed to cry?

Friends in London, I typed.

Ghiyath was a young man from Syria who arrived in the UK several months ago after a long and gruelling journey. Perhaps the hardship he'd been through was more than his heart could bear, because it suddenly stopped beating a few days ago as he lay on his bed, alone and without any witnesses. Like many of us, Ghiyath had no family here, and no friends. Tomorrow at 12.30 p.m, Ghiyath will be laid to rest in Nunhead Cemetery under the auspices of Lewisham Council. I will be present in accordance with the family's wishes. I invite anyone who can spare the time to join me in saying farewell to Ghiyath. Please share this post even if you're personally unable to attend.

After I had cried by the freezer, I wanted to go to bed. But then I remembered that the task awaiting me the following day wasn't going to be an easy one, and that I should prepare myself. It occurred to me that I needed to know a bit more about the young man whose burial I'd be attending, or rather, whose burial I was responsible for, at least in some sense. I found myself looking him up on Facebook. I typed *Ghiyath Abbas* into the search bar and a long list of profiles appeared, hundreds of them, all with the same name. It was confusing; they all seemed to come from Tartus. Some of them lived in London, some in Berlin, some in Istanbul, Beirut, Amman, Alexandria – every city you could think of. After checking a few of the profiles, I already felt drained and was about to give up. They were all of similar ages; they'd all travelled and been to a bunch of the same countries. But as I scrolled at random, I glimpsed a photo I recognized. It was the Ghiyath I was looking for, pictured with his arm around the friendly dolphin. It was the most real yet the most difficult to believe, like all true things. But apart from the picture, there wasn't much to be gleaned from his profile.

I rewrote the post a few times; it sounded stilted. I tried making it more formal, but then it came across as overdone. I settled on a final version without feeling satisfied. But this was the first time I'd organized the funeral of a person I didn't know, the first time I'd had to write a Facebook post inviting people to attend the burial of someone I'd never even met, and I thought people would probably appreciate how unusual the situation was and be able to overlook the awkwardness of what I'd written. I posted it on my page then turned off my phone. I was exhausted, and I didn't want to be kept awake by looking at people's comments.

I closed my eyes, but sleep wouldn't cooperate. I was anxious about what would happen when I got to work next morning, and panicky snatches of what had happened on the Tube kept coming back to me. Sometime around dawn, in a state between sleep and wakefulness, I saw something akin to a vision: myself standing in front of the boy's grave while thousands of mourners streamed into the cemetery, tens of thousands even, people of all colours and ages speaking all manner of languages, grief-stricken over the boy's death, weeping hot tears of sorrow for him, for their own loneliness and homesickness and for mine. I heard them saying it was the biggest funeral the city had ever seen; people would talk of it like they'd never talked of a funeral before. Strangers poured in from all directions to lay their fears down beside him and bury their pasts in his grave, finding comfort and consolation in each other. Everybody I'd met was there; the Cotton Man was playing some mournful yet joyous melody on an instrument, I spotted Pepsi without chalk on her face for the first time, and Kayode was beaming from ear to ear as tears coursed down his cheeks. I saw Service User A, alive, resting one arm on Ludmila's shoulder for support. The Free Hugs guy was giving out free hugs, as usual, to the funeralgoers, but they were sincere. James the beggar was there, smartly dressed and gleaming, looking slightly abashed as he watched me from a distance. He asked me for forgiveness, and I forgave him, though we exchanged no words. My auntie and her beloved Margaret Thatcher walked arm in arm, handing out ice cream to the children. I saw Potitsa approaching from a long way off and I waited for her; she put her arms around me, like in the old days, and whispered gently in my ear that it was time for us to forget. Then she turned to the crowds and said that the most dangerous things in this world were freezers and their icy ability to preserve anything and everything within them for ever.

8

The Ancient Egyptians believed a person had two souls. The *ka*, the person's companion on earth, resembled them exactly, while the *ba* was its heavenly counterpart and had wings that allowed it to fly back and forth. They also believed death was not soul leaving matter but soul leaving soul. While the *ka* remained close by to watch over the physical body, the *ba* took its leave when the time came and roamed abroad, seeking out its loved ones in places of remembrance. Sometimes it showed itself, and it always listened to them and spoke to their hearts. People never left their dead, and the dead never left their people; they kept each other close. The hardship of death, like the hardship of life, lay in a person's alienation from themselves and the soul's yearning for its companion soul. People were pained by the sufferings of the dead as they were by the sufferings of the living. Death was a long wait, or a long conflict, like life, and both came in many forms. Some people lived their whole lives with one soul instead of two, or died without their souls. Others were snubbed by their souls; some people's souls quarrelled among themselves during their lifetimes such that they only found peace in the grave.

Sometimes people's characters would change after death. A person's winged soul might be timid and introverted while its counterpart was sociable and outgoing, leaving the person wavering between the two until they died. After death a person could become closer to their loved ones, even spending more time with them than they had during their lives. In other cases a person's winged soul might wither away prematurely, and they would drag it limply behind them and die multiple slow, exhausting deaths. Then there were the impatient and restless ones who did it swiftly and surreptitiously so it was over in an instant.

My grandmother Badia's death was the long kind. Her celestial soul faded away, its wings broken, at least a decade before she died, and all that was left was the earthly companion which resembled her but didn't know much about her, and roamed among us like a ghost with no memory. People said all those dead bodies she'd seen in the morgue and the police station as a young woman had addled her mind, the doctors surmised it was Alzheimer's, the women in the family of her generation said it was the long wait she'd endured, and the priests at church declared that forgetting was a mercy from the Lord. She started off thinking all of her grandchildren were her first grandson and called them all Nayil, young and old alike. We went along with it; it would have been awful to make her suffer the shock all over again. We didn't tell her he'd gone to Hafr al-Batin and nobody had found his body. When the doctors came next, they said she would forget the present and return to the distant past, and so she did. She began to think every man she saw was the husband who'd gone away never to return, and she'd go running up to strangers in the street and kiss their hands, calling them by his name. The family locked her in the house so she wouldn't disgrace them. Doctors visited, and told the family to talk to her more and surround her with her loved ones so she'd remember their affection. Guests came and spoke to her about things from the past, but she wouldn't respond. We little ones tried to help too; we sat with her and told her all the stories she'd once told us, about Mother Ghoul and about kindly genies, and she'd smile as she listened, and sometimes cry. The priests nodded and said yes, she'd remember fantasy and forget reality, because that's what tortured souls did.

A few months after she was first locked up, she wandered into the reception room and tore open her robe to reveal her scrawny breasts, giggling as she capered around the guests. The doctors said it was senility, and prescribed new pills which she of course forgot to take. The family put a lock on the door to her room and kept her locked inside. This imprisonment was worse than the first. She forgot half the words she knew, and took to ripping apart the pillows and mattress with her nails. She'd pull out the cotton stuffing and throw lumps of it from the window at passers-by. People complained about the hailstorm of fluff, so the family nailed the window shut and bought her a sponge mattress.

Sooner or later they sent for the doctors again, because she'd shredded the mattress like she was excavating a grave and started chewing the bits of sponge. They had the intelligent idea of removing the bed and replacing it with a wooden board. When on the first night she started chewing the edges like a mouse, it was clear things were getting worse. The church advised that everything be removed from her room, and the doctor had no objection, so the family acted on their advice. When they opened her bedroom door once a day, we'd find her curled up on the tiles in a ball. We talked to her but she didn't hear us. We touched her but she didn't feel us. We told her the stories but she never responded. Over time everyone got tired, and we forgot about her there in the bedroom, just as we forgot most of her stories.

When her *ba* left her frail body, she was laid out on the settee in the sitting room, the same position she used to lie in to have her nap. She stayed there for four whole days, as her will had specified. The neighbours didn't understand, and the doctors warned that the smell would be strong and harmful. The priests were dumbfounded; the soul left the house after three days, and they themselves had visited to send it on its way, so why the wait? My aunts bathed her once a day, and wiped away the foam at her mouth with a handkerchief every few hours. On the day she was to be buried, Helena, the eldest, arrived. 'What will people say?' she scolded them.

I was sitting on the floor near the door and I watched as she did everything. She undressed Grandmother and tossed her black clothes onto the tiles, then picked her up like a child and placed her into the big tin basin. She bathed her in cologne, gently massaging her body like a bride before her wedding night. She took out some bright, spring-coloured clothes, which Grandmother hadn't worn ever since she

154

put on the black garb of widowhood, and dressed her in all her gold. With an ivory comb, she combed her hair out on her lap and rubbed it with oil. It was silver like moonlight and as rough as her life had been, as long and tangled as a rocky path. Aunt Helena's final touches were a dab of lipstick and some rouge on her cheeks. Then she sat her in the big chair by the window where she always used to sit, and tuned the radio to the station that played the songs she liked. People filed in one by one to pay their respects, each placing a last kiss on her shining forehead. Looking peaceful and calm, she appeared to be smiling contentedly at them. At the end of the night, the aunts looked around at one another.

'That's how you do a funeral,' said Helena proudly. 'Or better not at all.'

As I woke up, I was thinking about my grandmother's funeral. That was when I had realized how much the dead have to put up with when it comes to funerals, and that death is by no means the end of their labour. So I tried not to think about what was awaiting me at the office, and to put Service User A and Kayode out of my mind. The boy's funeral and burial, and the attendees, deserved all my attention right now.

I stretched out an arm and ran my fingertips over the bedside table, like I did each morning, until they closed around my phone. Bringing it to my face, I quickly flicked through the notifications. It was disheartening. There weren't many comments on the Facebook post I'd made about the funeral, maybe twenty, almost all of which were simply condolences. Two people said they'd try to make it to the cemetery but might arrive late. Three had shared the post on their own pages. In my Messenger inbox was a message from someone I didn't know, saying he was very moved by my post and wanted to attend but couldn't because it was during working hours, and asking if there was anything he could do to help. Twenty comments, thirty-five likes, one message and three shares: all that was left of a whole life. I thought that was pretty disappointing, but it was better than nothing, I suppose.

It was an appropriate day to wear an ironed shirt, even a full suit, and this cheered me up a bit. As long as one could find an opportunity to wear a suit, iron their shirt and polish their shoes, then life was worth living, or at least meant something. People at work might be a little bit disconcerted, but who cared. It was not unlikely that today would be my last day, so I might as well say my goodbyes looking sharp, with as much dignity as possible. I only owned one suit, which I'd brought from Cairo when I first arrived, so I didn't take long getting dressed. The jacket was a bit small, as I'd expected it would be after ten years; it was tight in the shoulders, and I couldn't move properly, but I reminded myself suits weren't meant to be comfortable. I was out of the house in five minutes. I wanted to get to work on time and I didn't feel like getting the Tube after what had happened yesterday, so I needed to set out early. God knows how long it would take by bus.

The traffic was moving at a reasonable pace given it was rush hour, and the bus trundled along slowly without any hold-ups. I had the best seat on board – top floor, at the front, and on the sunny side too – and I looked out at the street from above, imagining it was a stage and I a spectator watching from the dress circle. Not much was happening, and the scenery was minimal: children were walking to school, with their identical uniforms and harmonious chaos, while adults made their way to work. Rigid monotony that spoke of discipline and determination. It struck me that none of them knew a thing about a poor boy called Ghiyath who would be buried today. For the rest of the way, I gazed out across the endless city blocks of Victorian terraces, one after the other, and as usual it had a soothing, reassuring effect. On second thoughts it was actually more like looking into a peep box than being at the theatre.

The bus pulled up at a stop and lots of schoolchildren got out. I noticed a homeless shelter close to the school; it didn't have a sign saying that was what it was, but I knew by instinct and a little guesswork. I can't explain it exactly. There's a kind of knowledge that a person picks up through experience without noticing. But when two people came out of the main entrance, I knew from their appearance I was right. The bus moved on, and although I didn't know the route or the street names, it was all familiar to me, and stories flickered before my eyes every few hundred metres. In ten years here I'd been inside every homeless hostel in the borough; I'd seen hundreds of temporary accommodation cells, met hundreds of tenants, and heard their backstories. What I knew of their pasts was far less than they wanted the world to know, but more than I could bear.

Now the bus was creeping along and as I stared out, I could see through walls to the things happening inside them that other passengers couldn't see. I wasn't sure if I was lucky or unlucky. Looking to the other side of the bus, I noticed a young woman smiling to herself as she listened to music. She didn't know. I envied her.

As we passed the hostel where Service User A had lived, I saw two police officers were removing the plastic tape that ringed the premises. They must have finished the forensic investigation. Everything looked normal from the outside – it could have been any ordinary day.

'Gary's waiting for you,' said the receptionist curtly as I came through the door. My heart had begun to race as I neared the office, and she didn't give me the chance to catch my breath. 'He wants you to meet him in the conference room straight away.'

From her formal manner, I realized she knew everything. Perhaps everyone knew. It wasn't the sort of thing you could keep secret. I felt relieved: soon the matter would be settled, and I'd know my fate. No more waiting and confusion.

The receptionist eyed me quizzically, still frowning. 'Why are you wearing a suit, anyway?' she asked, in the same formal tone that people put on to conceal cruelty. 'You won the lottery? Or got yourself a real job?'

'No, I've got a funeral today.'

She laughed. I wasn't sure if she thought I was joking, or was simply amused by the irony of what I'd said. I smiled and walked past her desk, into the office. 'Good luck,' she called from behind me, in a tone that sounded partly pitying, partly callous. I was going to need it, I thought.

But as I reached the conference room, I realized it was too late now for even luck to help me. Through the glass wall I could see Gary looking grim. On the table in front of him was a cup of tea and a blue folder surrounded by loose papers.

'Come in,' said Gary. 'Sorry to get you in so early. You probably need a tea or coffee.'

He was adhering strictly to British work etiquette, which required that everything begin and end with an apology; the more apologies there were, the worse the situation was. I shook my head and asked him to go ahead, opening my eyes wide to show I was paying attention.

'I imagine you know why I've asked you to come in.'

A half-laugh slipped awkwardly out before I could stifle the other half. They were just too British, these statements that denied a thing in order to affirm it. I could only assume he meant the opposite. When I first came to the UK I couldn't get my head around these turns of phrase and their counter-intuitive meanings, or rather their double meanings. It was months before I could distinguish between statements that meant what they meant and statements that did not mean what they meant. Over time, this came more easily to me, and sometimes I even managed to do it myself. People here preferred to speak in this inverted fashion; to convey meanings directly and nakedly was considered indiscreet and impolite other than among close friends. I nodded again in response, assuming my own role in the game. I had to admit it could be fun; there was something poetic about utterances that hovered at the edges of meaning, frolicking in its hinterland.

'As your line manager,' Gary began, 'I wanted to be the first one to tell you. The day before yesterday, you conducted a home visit to a woman known to us as Service User A, who was temporarily housed in a hostel. I'm very sorry to tell you that she died in tragic circumstances a few hours after you'd left.'

It wasn't obvious whether I should feign shock or sadness, another pair I struggled to tell apart. Luckily I guessed Gary wouldn't tolerate any excessive displays of emotion in the office anyway, and instead I made a perplexed face, pretending I was trying to take in what he'd said. I didn't utter a word. This was really bad, and I didn't want to make it worse.

'As you know, the police have opened an investigation.'

Gary had switched strategy. Now he was saying that I did know. This was surprising. Maybe it was a trap? I'd have to use one of those lines that said something and meant nothing.

'Of course, the police would have to investigate something like this.'

Gary sat up straight. 'Something like what?' he asked, his earlier mildness replaced by an aggressive tone.

I was ready with an answer, but the sudden transformation of his features made me hesitate. 'I mean when a person dies in tragic circumstances,' I said, being careful to reproduce his words exactly; he would pounce at the first mistake I made. 'Isn't that what you said?'

'Listen, there's no need for all this,' he snapped. 'I'm going to tell you something in a personal capacity. You know you made a mistake, and a pretty big one.'

Gary sounded angry, and his Scottish accent was more noticeable now he was speaking so vehemently. He'd dropped the forced-sounding English accent he normally used when he was being serious, and this was a relief, because it meant we could stop beating around the bush. Everyone could show their hand. I nodded ever so slightly, too slightly to be readable.

'Why did you tell the poor woman she'd never get permanent accommodation?'

I was about to object and make clear I'd said nothing; it was Kayode who'd said that. But he didn't give me a chance.

'There's nothing more important than transparency. That's what we believe in this office. You know that. As local authority employees, our job is to be transparent with the public. And you understand very well that transparency requires us not to tell tenants the truth. Transparency requires discretion, quite simply because we can't be certain of anything. The government raises the State Pension age every year. Do you know when you'll be able to retire? Of course you don't, and neither do I. Every few months we get another notice about wage cuts or benefit reductions, or they go changing the eligibility criteria. Next week they might change how people qualify for social housing. Our job doesn't require truths, it requires procedures. The procedures are the only truth that is relevant to us.'

While Gary took a sip of tea, I seized my chance to defend myself. 'But I didn't say anything!' I protested.

Gary pretended not to hear and carried on. 'Do you know what the tenants call us?' he asked. His tone of voice was softer now, but the anger in his face was clearer. 'The "yellow form guys". Our job is to fill in yellow forms, and that's it. We don't make decisions, we don't inform

161

people what decisions have been made, we're just the yellow form guys. That's it. The day before yesterday, a tenant came into the office with the results of a blood test showing that his white blood cell count was below five hundred. He'd found out his HIV had developed into AIDS. He was delighted it was finally official, because it meant he'd jump to the front of the housing queue and finally move into permanent accommodation. I could have said, "Congratulations! You've got AIDS. Wonderful news!" But I didn't, because my job is transparency. I took out the Health and Housing Change in Circumstances form and asked him to fill it in and attach an original copy of the medical report. You know why I did that? Because these illnesses are just numbers to the state. Tomorrow they might change it and say that to qualify as AIDS the count has to be four hundred, or three hundred, or God knows what. They're all just numbers, and they could change at any time. The only thing that doesn't change here is that we can't be sure of anything.'

'I told you, Gary,' I interrupted. 'I didn't say anything.' I'd had enough of being lectured. The woman had already killed herself; there was nothing I could do about it now.

His eyes were blazing as he opened the blue folder, flicked through it until he found a piece of paper and waved it in front of me.

'Yes you did. This is a statement from Service User A's son. See for yourself.' Gary pushed the piece of paper towards me and pointed to the second paragraph. I could hardly believe what I was seeing. It made no sense.

ON THE GREENWICH LINE

My mother called me at around 12.30 p.m. I was not expecting her to call. She had not been in contact with us since she came out of the psychiatric hospital. She sounded quiet and more cheerful than usual. She said two of the yellow form guys had visited her. They asked her funny questions and showed her funny pictures. One of them spoke Arabic. I couldn't understand from her what the purpose of the visit was, but she said that the visitors were honest with her and that it was the first time anyone had spoken to her so transparently. They told her, 'You will never get a flat, so there's no point waiting any longer.' She decided that the time had come to make up with me and move back in. She had found waiting very difficult, and she said that having her hopes kept in the air was like being suspended in Barzakh [NB, interpreter explained that in Islam this is a place between life and the hereafter, akin to purgatory]. Now, thanks to the visit from the two men, she felt like she had lost all hope and could have her life back. I was glad to hear this and we agreed I'd go over after work to talk to her. But then things happened.

I read the paragraph again; there was nothing else. I looked at Gary, waiting for him to say something, but he didn't.

'That's it? So why did she kill herself?'

Gary shifted in his seat, put down the pen he'd been gripping throughout and stared at me in genuine surprise. 'Kill herself?'

Kayode had been wrong. Our anxieties about Service User A were completely unfounded. We'd dreamed the whole thing up. Gary told me that the boiler room had exploded, causing a fire which affected her room only. She'd been the only one who'd died, possibly as a result of her underlying health conditions. A handful of other residents had suffered superficial and moderate burns.

I was overwhelmed by a muddle of contradictory emotions that I struggled, as usual, to tell apart or disambiguate into single feelings. I no longer needed to fear for my job. That was cause for joy, or at least relief. The woman had died, and that was sad, but it was someone else's problem now. The receptionist at the hostel had been suspended and a review was being conducted of the performance of the site maintenance contractor. The boiler had blown up just after we'd left, and I wasn't sure whether I should be glad I hadn't died or shaken it had been such a close shave. I'd survived by pure chance. It was sheer coincidence I was alive. A stroke of luck had extracted me from the fetters of probability. I reflected that perhaps my long-standing inability to identify my emotions wasn't down to some psychological issue but a natural response to the way the world worked. How was a person supposed to feel about surviving? Surviving meant others not surviving. Surviving meant the implicit, permanent chance one would not survive other than by good fortune.

'Do you know what's up with Kayode?' Gary went on. 'Has he lost his mind? His boss rang me this morning, says he's denying he visited Service User A. It sounds like he's in a real pickle. The security cameras show him entering the building with you at eleven then leaving an hour later. He clearly doesn't realize you can't lie these days, at least not when there isn't someone who wants to believe you. I'd suggest you steer clear of him.'

I nodded and made a mystified face like I knew nothing about it. Then he commented in surprise on my suit, and I told him I'd need to make my excuses in an hour, to attend a funeral. He gave a sympathetic look and said there was no need to stay; I could head off now if I wanted.

'It's a shock to survive something like that,' said Gary, more kindly than usual. 'You'll need a bit of time to take it in.'

Nunhead Cemetery is a large cemetery, one of London's 'Magnificent Seven', so it was for the best that I set out much earlier than planned. I'd never been there before and I was right to be worried I'd have difficulty finding the Islamic section. Getting to the cemetery itself was easy; a quick Tube and a short train ride to a station five minutes' walk away. I wasn't nervous about taking the Underground as I had been in the morning; I read *Metro* and was distracted by a piece about a German family who were suing Facebook after the death of their daughter. They wanted to force the company to hand over her account password. I didn't know what to think: the family's reasoning, that legally they were her inheritors, was compelling, but the company argued that memory, like history, could not be posthumously transferred to a new owner and should remain available to all. I found this more convincing, and reflected that US corporations could be rather romantic after all, just like the rest of us. Lost in thought, I would have missed my stop had the announcement not roused me just in time to get out at London Bridge. I was supposed to take a train from there, but when I got to the station, it was full of police officers wielding machine guns, and I panicked at the sight of them searching people. Someone said there'd been a bomb scare but nothing had been found. I hurried to my platform, grinning but shaken; it was my second near miss that day. How many strokes of luck did a person get? I wondered nervously if I'd used all mine up.

'Hello there, you must be here for Ghiyath's funeral. I'm Tariq.'

I arrived five minutes late. I'd got lost in the vast cemetery, going back on myself several times because I couldn't imagine that the Islamic section would be right behind the chapel, of all places. I kept walking past it, not noticing that all the graves faced east, and I probably would have missed it again had not a short, rotund, sixty-something man with dyed-black hair and a thick moustache hailed me in a childlike voice and saved me another lap. He held out a large bouquet of yellow flowers and told me they were for the departed. He spoke in English, but I guessed from his accent that Arabic was his native language, and asked him if he spoke it.

'I heard about the funeral from a friend,' the man said, ignoring my question as if he hadn't heard. 'He saw your post on Facebook. Am I right in thinking this is your first time?'

I had no idea what he meant, and for some reason his dyed hair, which glinted blue in the sun, got on my nerves. 'My first time at what?' I asked with a note of derision.

The man smiled, took two steps towards me, and placed his hand on my shoulder. 'I've been attending the funerals of people I don't know for years. Many of them have nobody to arrange their funerals. I can tell you've never done this before. Ten years ago, I watched a Channel 4 documentary about a group of ladies in America who organized funerals for soldiers killed in Iraq that had no families. I'm from Iraq, so I thought I should do something similar. I found out that hundreds of people die here without anyone to attend their funeral – much more than anywhere else. At first I started with Iraqis, and then I expanded my activities to include other Arab nationalities. So I'm very busy. It takes up most of my time now I'm retired. You know, each one of us has to do what they can to help build a better world, and let me tell you this: there's no place for mercy in a world where the dead are not respected or given the send-off they deserve. I've devoted the rest of my life to this sacred mission.'

The man talked for what felt like hours, an obsessive gleam in his eyes, about the adventures he'd had performing his mission, interspersed with his memories of Iraq. He'd been a military engineer until the Gulf War, when he fled the country. Some of the things he said were brilliant, though he was clearly unhinged.

'At the gates of the grave, I fight loneliness on its last battleground! I snatch its victims from its talons!'

A lot of what he was saying was pure fantasy, but it was entertaining, and a couple of times I had to laugh out loud. He mentioned in passing that he was a communist, which explained some of his more memorable claims. He was convinced that what he was doing was vital in forging a path to a radiant socialist future.

'Loneliness is the weapon of capitalism, and its defeat will herald the victory of socialism.'

I felt sorry for him, and amazed by his singular devotion. He'd been talking for a very long time, but no other mourners appeared, and neither did the body. I tried calling the Cotton Man a few times to check there hadn't been a change of plan, but the line just rang and rang before going dead. My fellow funeralgoer wasn't perturbed, and told me that arrangements often got thrown out by a few hours, so I shouldn't worry. 'You know, I was at the funeral of another young man from Syria yesterday,' he went on. 'There was only one other mourner, and we waited two hours. The other man was very odd, and he said some very funny things. He was a journalist, also from Syria, and he'd come because he wanted to write a piece about the dead man. He was disappointed, because the only story he ended up with was mine! He smoked like a chimney, like he was puffing out his frustration with every drag, and he said all sorts of ludicrous things. Like "I'd love to be the next García Márquez!" You know, that Colombian writer. Or Argentinian? I said he might be setting his sights a bit high. But then he said he thought he was more talented than García Márquez, the only problem was that he wasn't such a lowlife! Can you believe that?'

Hours had passed, and clouds had begun to gather above our heads, covering the sun. I was starting to worry. The man's story was enjoyable, but I was getting hungry and cold, and it looked like it was about to rain.

'He said García Márquez was a pimp, shamelessly making money like that off the back of writing about dictatorship and suffering. Said he wished he could be just as unscrupulous instead of having a conscience. The more people died in Syria, the more articles he had to write and the more he got paid. That tortured him.'

My phone rang and I leaped to answer it, thinking it would be the Cotton Man. But it was Kayode. There were multiple missed calls from him. I wasn't feeling calm enough to answer.

The man was still talking all the while, switching nimbly from one topic to another. He clearly didn't often find some-one who would listen to him. 'You see, I became a com-munist in Iraq,' he ploughed on, 'because I wanted to rebel against my parents. Since moving here, I've become very Muslim, for exactly the same reason. Bloody-mindedness. I never miss a prayer! That's what Iraqi communists are like. If you visit Marx's grave, up in Highgate, you'll find all the leaders of the Communist Party buried next to him, with Quranic verses on their gravestones.'

A light rain began to fall. It was after five. I tried one last time to call the Cotton Man, but to no avail. I was starving and exhausted.

'So you see, it was the Iraqis who brought Islam to Marx's grave.'

He chuckled at his own joke, and I chuckled with him. It began to rain harder. It was late, and we decided to leave.

ACKNOWLEDGEMENTS

Part of this translation was undertaken while in residence at Nawat Fes, the artist residency programme of the American Language Center Fes.

THE PEIRENE SUBSCRIPTION

Since 2011, Peirene Press has run a subscription service which has brought a world of translated literature to thousands of readers. We seek out great stories and original writing from across the globe, and work with the best translators to bring these books into English – before sending each one to our subscribers ahead of publication. All of our books are beautifully designed collectible paperback editions, printed in the UK using sustainable materials.

Join our reading community today and subscribe to receive three or six books a year, as well as invitations to events and launch parties and discounts on all our titles. We also offer a gift subscription, so you can share your literary discoveries with friends and family.

A one-year subscription costs £38 for three books, or £68 for six books. Postage costs apply.

www.peirenepress.com/subscribe

'The foreign literature specialist'

The Sunday Times

'A class act'

The Guardian